NOT LIKE HER

H.K. CHRISTIE

KEEKSTAR
MEDIA

ALSO BY H.K. CHRISTIE

The Selena Bailey Novella Series

Not Like Her, Book 1 is the first book in the suspenseful Selena Bailey Novella series. If you like thrilling twists, dark tension, and smart and driven women, then you'll love this dark mystery series.

One In Five, Book 2

On The Rise, Book 3

The Unbreakable Series

The Unbreakable Series is a heart-warming women's fiction series, inspired by true events. If you like journeys of self-discovery, wounded heroines, and laugh-or-cry moments, you'll love the Unbreakable Series

We Can't Be Broken, Book 0

Where I'm Supposed To Be, Book 1

Change of Plans, Book 2

For Gianna

1

S elena turned up the volume on her iPod. It had become increasingly difficult to study with Mom's latest boyfriend, Fox, around. *Ick.* The guy couldn't be any less aptly named. He looked less like a fox and more like a gerbil. Fat and hairy with beady eyes. The couple's nightly ritual of getting drunk and fighting was really starting to get on her nerves. Why would you want to date somebody when all you do is fight? What about flowers? Sweet nothings? Grand gestures? Where was the honeymoon phase people always talked about?

Mom and Fox had been dating for an entire month and Selena didn't think they ever had a day where they didn't fight. But it wasn't anything new. It was Mom's MO. *Modis Operandi.* Fox was just the latest in a long list of asshole boyfriends she had brought home. It was the fate of an alcoholic, Selena supposed. *Note to self. Don't be an alcoholic.*

Her mother was one of the reasons Selena never touched the stuff. Even when her friends were partying, she was full-on abstinent. Selena did everything in her power to not to turn into her mother. Debbie Bailey was burned out at thirty-five, barely scraping by with a dead-end job at the grocery outlet and dating losers like Fox.

Seven more months, Selena thought as she searched for a song loud enough to drown out the banging cupboards. In seven months she'd be eighteen years old and off to college, far away from the dump they were living in. It was times like these when she pondered what it would be like to have a "normal" family. She supposed she'd never know.

A bump on the wall forced her to sit up straight on her bed. It was going to be a rough one tonight. Instead of turning up the volume further and blowing out her eardrums, Selena shut her book and shoveled her study notes and textbook into her backpack. She had an AP Chemistry test the next day and she needed to do well. College applications were looming, and she needed to secure her grades before she started writing her essays. She was already at risk of not being able to get into any of her first-choice schools. Not to mention her senior project. No, she certainly didn't have time to deal with Debbie and Fox.

Selena slipped on her shoes and made her way over to the window. She slid it open at a snail's pace and dropped her bag outside before climbing over the sill in hopes of escaping unnoticed.

She hadn't felt the wrath of Fox. Not yet. Selena's approach with the newest guy was to avoid at all possible costs.

Once outside she gently slid the window shut, dual-strapped her backpack, and headed for the street. On the main strip, she hurried down the busy road, careful to avoid eye contact with any pedestrians or drivers, at least one of whom always seemed to think she was looking for a good time. She never was.

By fate or chance, she reached the Starbucks safely and without any kind of harassment. No hoots or hollers. No "give us a smile, little lady." It must be her lucky day.

She pushed open the door and inhaled the aroma of fresh-ground coffee beans before she approached the barista at the counter, a middle-aged woman with wire rim glasses and a round middle, mostly hidden by her kelly-green apron. She asked, "What can I get you tonight, Selena?"

Selena was a regular at the coffee shop, considering she often needed to escape from the apartment to focus on studying and/or her sanity. Both were her top priority at the moment.

"Let's see. I'll have the Pumpkin Spice Frappuccino. 'Tis the season."

"It is. Don't you love it?" The woman mouthed *Pumpkin Spice Frapp* as she keyed the order into the register.

Selena passed a crumpled five-dollar bill to the barista and gave her best attempt at a friendly smile. She wasn't sure how convincing she was. What did she have to smile about anyway?

She had to pay nearly five dollars of her hard-earned money for a beverage. After taxes, that was nearly an hour's worth of work at her hostess job. Sure, they were tasty, but she needed that five dollars. She didn't work twenty hours a week for nothing. She needed money for things like clothes, make-up, fun, college, and who was she kidding, Frappucinos. It wasn't like Mom and Dad were chipping in. She hadn't even seen her dad in five years. She didn't know where he was either. If she had to guess, it was somewhere shooting up.

Sugar fix in hand, she found a table in the corner farthest away from any other patrons in the large coffee shop. In her direct line of sight, she eyed a group of boys, probably a little older than she was. Maybe in college. They were checking her out like she was a gazelle and they were the mighty lions. *This isn't Animal Planet, so mind your business. Okay?* She was overly tired of boys who seemed to prioritize hooking up over all else. *Get some goals already.* She couldn't wait to get out of this town.

She refocused on her backpack and pulled out her book. It landed on the table with a thump. She shrugged and took a sip of her pumpkin spice goodness and decided it was worthy of her precious dollars. It was the one joy she had in this life other than window shopping and hanging out with her bestie, Alida.

Before she could crack open the book, one of the boys appeared at her table. *Great. Why does every man who sees a woman sitting by herself think she needs company? She doesn't.* Her attempt at putting out the "closed" sign by wearing baggy jeans and over-sized sweatshirt, hiding her petite and slightly curvy frame, with no make-up and a messy bun didn't seem to compute. Did she really look like she wanted to chit chat? *Uh, no.*

"Hi, is anyone sitting here?" He grinned and a row of perfectly straight teeth glared at her.

She scowled. "No."

He ruffled his shaggy, blond hair to the side. "May I?"

She smirked. "I prefer that you didn't. I need to study."

"Okay, sorry to bother you. My name is Zeek, by the way. What's yours?"

She pursed her lips. "Not interested." She diverted her gaze from the tall, and sort of hot, guy. She flipped open the cover of her AP Chemistry textbook and started skimming the page until he got the hint and removed himself from her vicinity. She wasn't in the mood for some random guy to hit on her. Plus, she had a test the next morning and she needed an A to keep her GPA up. *Goals, people, goals.*

It was nearly ten o'clock when Selena approached her first-floor apartment. She hiked through the bushes to her bedroom window and slid it open, careful not to make any noise or arouse any suspicion. The window cracked open and Selena took note of the silence inside. Not a sound. *Score. They're already passed out.* Mom and Fox's relationship basically consisted of the pattern of get drunk, fight, fuck, and then pass out. *Romantic.* Mom always pestered her as to why she never had a boyfriend. Hello, if that's what a boyfriend was like, *no, thanks.*

She lowered her backpack over the window seal and climbed over. She stood up straight and shut the window, glancing around her small, tidy room. Nothing was out of place, but her door was slightly ajar. *That's odd.* Had her mom come looking for her? She slipped off her black-and-white checkered Vans and shuffled over to her door. She stepped back and scrunched up her face. What was that smell? Urine? Crap? A mix?

Selena tiptoed into the hall. The smell appeared to be coming from the living room. She covered her nose and mouth with her hand as she continued on into the living room. She flicked on the light switch and gasped. Her heart thudded in her chest as she rushed over to the body lying motionless on the floor next to the sofa. The face was so badly beaten she could only recognize it was her mother because of the bleached blond hair and the sagging Betty Boop tattoo on her chest. She cried, "Mom?"

No response.

Selena's hands shook as she pulled her cellphone from her back pocket and dialed 9-1-1.

"9-1-1 what's your emergency?"

Selena stared at her mother. "It's my mom. She's been beaten. There are ... There's marks on her neck. I don't know if she's breathing. Please hurry. Please." Tears streamed down Selena's face as she searched for any sign of life.

2

Selena slumped into the brown cloth chair in the crowded hospital emergency room. She fidgeted in an attempt to get comfortable, but it was impossible. It had been hours and she'd received zero news about her mother. She had no idea if she was alive or dead. She stared at the floor to avoid stares from the dozen or so others waiting in the room. A tap on her shoulder forced her to swivel around. A nurse with wide eyes and a ruddy complexion said, "Selena?"

She shifted upward. "Yes. Is it my mom? Is she okay?"

"She's awake. You can see her now. I'll show you to her room."

Selena slipped out of her chair, grabbed her coat, and followed the woman through the double doors and down the hall. The air was frigid and smelled like antiseptic and sickness. They passed several open doors full of patients in blue and white gowns before the nurse stopped and pointed. "Second bed."

"Thanks."

Selena wrapped her arms around herself as she entered the room. She passed the first patient, currently yelling obscenities at another nurse, and then stopped at the foot of her mother's bed. She looked small and fragile. Beaten and battered. "Hi, Mom. Are you okay?"

Her mother rubbed at the gauze around her head and spoke slowly. "I'll be fine. The doctor is supposed to be in soon to talk to me."

Selena forced back the tears as she scooted closer to the top of the bed. "What happened?"

Her mother's dull brown eyes were filled with sadness. Her voice shook as she spoke. "I don't know. All I remember is waking up in here. They haven't told me anything."

Selena studied her mother. It made her stomach turn to see the gifts Fox had given her. Bruises, a pair of black eyes, and a necklace of fingerprints.

Selena was about to enquire further when a tall, lanky man wearing blue scrubs and a white coat entered. He tipped his head to Selena before focusing on her mother. "Deborah, my name is Dr. Fransia, I was the one to take care of you when you arrived. Do you remember anything about your attack?"

Debbie shook her head.

He spoke with an authoritative tone. "That's not terribly uncommon. Due to your high blood alcohol content, memory loss is typical. It appears you were struck several times in the face and head and were strangled, but we don't see anything to be too worried about. You likely passed out due to the alcohol and not the injuries you sustained. Most of your wounds appear superficial and should heal up in no time."

Nothing to be too worried about? Selena couldn't believe what she was hearing. Selena tried to accept the doctor's explanation, but something was different about her mother's supposed drunken black out. Her mother had passed out plenty of times in the past, but she always seemed to remember the day before, or at least most of it. Her sober descriptions of events were hazy, but they were still descriptions. No, this was most definitely different. *Why couldn't the doctor see that?*

Selena's pulse raced. She stared at the doctor. "Are you sure? She's never had complete memory loss before. She always remembers something."

The wrinkled old man gave her a patronizing smile. "Bits and pieces may come back over time. I assure you, this is normal for the amount of alcohol she consumed. And you're her daughter, I presume?"

Selena stared at him in disbelief. "Yes."

"Do the two of you live alone?"

"Yes."

" Your mom is going to need to rest up, but she'll be okay. I promise. A police officer will be in shortly to take her statement. Did you see what happened?"

"No, I just found her, like that."

He nodded. "Hmm. We'll discharge her shortly. She'll need plenty of rest. Now, both of you take care."

Before Selena or her mother could say another word, he rushed out of the room. Bedside manner, much? She gazed back at her mom and arched her tweezed brows. "You really don't remember anything?"

"No."

"Do you remember what time Fox left?"

Debbie's eyes widened. "Fox was over?"

Selena's mouth dropped open. She didn't remember Fox had been there? How much of her mother's memory had she lost? "Yes."

Panic spread across Debbie's battered face. "Don't tell the police, okay?"

Don't tell the police that Fox had savagely attacked her? Selena couldn't believe her mother wouldn't press charges. She had to have known Fox did this. Who else would have or could have done this? If she didn't report him, he could come back and finish what he'd started. Maybe next time he'd come after Selena too. Had he come into her room looking for her after he'd attacked her mother? Terror seeped into her bones. What if he came back?

When the police officers came to question her mother, Debbie gave them the same nonstory she'd told Selena. Selena sat quietly until it was her turn to explain how she had found her. Neither of the women mentioned Fox's name.

3

The barista chirped, "Your regular?"

Selena nodded. The barista asked, "Is everything okay, hon?"

Everything was just super. She attempted to sound cheerful. "Just a rough night, that's all. I'm fine." Rough *like I thought my mom was dead.* Rough *like she was rushed to the hospital and I had to wait to find out if she was going to die.* Despite the doctor's assurances, they hadn't left the hospital until nearly nine in the morning, and Selena had managed only a short nap before her restlessness drove her to leave the apartment. Just another day in the life of Selena Bailey. Shitty parents. Shitty life. *Nobody ever said life was fair.* She suspected that was the one true thing her mother had ever said to her. It was a common phrase out of her mother's lips. "Grow up, kid. Nobody ever said life was fair."

She supposed she should be grateful that her mother didn't die yesterday. Despite the fact Debbie had insisted that she didn't know who had attacked her, she had to know it was likely her jerk boyfriend, Fox. He had pushed her around since they'd met, but never anything like this. This was vicious and savage. How could her mother be so stupid as to keep dating someone who physically abused her? What if she didn't survive the next beating?

Selena wondered if she'd even miss her. Her mother was hardly ever at home and when she was, she was preoccupied with the latest loser or harassing Selena about not giving her any of *her* money or complaining about having to raise her. *Raise me. Now there's a joke.*

But if she was gone, what would happen to Selena? She wouldn't be eighteen for another seven months. Would she become a ward of the state and have to go into foster care or a group home? She wasn't trying to gain admission to either institution. No, she needed her mom to stay alive for at least seven more months. Was it terrible that she thought that way about her own mother? Was she a bad person or just practical?

As it was with Debbie's new look, we'll call it Battered Woman, would she even be able to go to work? How would they make rent this month if not? Selena had a good idea of how. Her mother would "borrow" money from Selena again. From her college fund. It wasn't much, but it was something and it was *hers*.

She took a seat at a table for two and nursed her drug of choice. She supposed she could be consuming far worse than a Pumpkin Spice Frappuccino. She stared at her drink as she sipped from the green straw. She was tired. She was pissed off. She'd missed her test and hoped Alida would arrive soon so that she could go home and get some sleep.

She would've told her to meet her at school the next day, but she wanted Alida's notes from their shared classes and some insight on their AP Chemistry test for when she took the makeup exam. Assuming she could take the makeup. Her mother would have to write her a note to excuse her absence, which meant they'd have to have an actual conversation. *She couldn't wait.* She twirled around her straw but froze when she heard a semi-familiar voice. "We meet again."

Selena glanced up, straw still in her mouth. He was cute. Had he been this cute the night before? He continued. "You're Ms. Not Interested, right?"

Funny too?

Was it her exhaustion that was finding this man child somewhat appealing? At the very minimum it was clouding her judgment. She really needed to get some sleep. Against all of her common sense, she said, "Actually, it's Selena. Not Interested is my middle name."

He slid into the chair she'd reserved for Alida. His eyes twinkled. "Nice to meet you, Selena. I do think you look much more like a Selena than a Not Interested. I'm Zeek." He extended his hand across the table.

Selena hesitated but eventually gave in and shook his hand. "Nice to meet you." *Was it?*

"No books today?"

"Not today." She sipped her beverage and stared skeptically into his pale blue eyes.

He tapped his finger on his chin. "Let me guess, you're a senior at Grapton Hill High?"

"Guilty." *Not impressed.* It didn't take a rocket scientist to figure that out considering that there was only one high school in town.

"I'm at Cal State East Bay. I'm majoring in computer science with a minor in business. I love it. College. Having my own apartment. It's the best."

That was Selena's dream. Zeek was living the life she wanted. She couldn't wait to be done with high school. Done with her mother. Done with this crappy town. Zeek was the first guy she'd ever met who seemed to have goals beyond trying to break their beer pong record. A college man. Maybe he wasn't so bad after all.

Before Selena could ask him any questions, her best friend approached, hand on hip. "Hey, I thought you were saving me a seat?"

She was about to explain when Zeek slipped off the chair and said, "It's my fault. I'm so sorry. I was so captivated by your friend here, I had to talk to her. I had no idea she was saving the seat for you. Please, sit and forgive me. I don't want to intrude."

Alida eyed Zeek and then Selena before accepting the seat. "Uh-huh."

He gazed at Selena. "It was great meeting you."

She tried to suppress a smile as she waved.

He took a step and then turned around. He beamed at Selena. "If you're here tomorrow around six, maybe we can talk again?"

Selena felt her cheeks burn as she attempted to be coy. "I *might* be here." *I'll definitely be here.*

"I hope you are. Tuesdays are a terrible day for heartbreak." He winked and sauntered out of the coffee shop.

Selena watched him leave. He was confident, she'd give him that.

Alida waved her hand in front of Selena. "Earth to Selena."

"Oh, sorry. Were you saying something?"

"No, but did you just make a date with some random guy? He's cute but a little, I don't know, slimy."

"You think he's slimy?" Had she been too tired to notice?

"Oh, I don't know. Maybe just a bit eager for my taste. He seems to be quite enamored with you, though."

She might just be a little enamored with him too, though she didn't know why. There was just something about him that made her body tingle all over.

4

Selena applied gold shadow on her lids, accentuating her light brown eyes, before dabbing on a thin layer of peach lip gloss and smacking her lips together. Her dark chestnut hair flowed past her shoulders and she wore a tight sweater and pair of skinny jeans with flats. She grabbed her coat from the entryway closet and slipped it on, glancing over at her mother sitting on the sofa watching television. Her face was now a mish mash of blue, purple, yellow, and green. It wasn't a good look for her. Or anyone. They hadn't talked about the incident, mostly because they didn't talk about much. She pondered for a moment what it was like to be Debbie. A string of drunk boyfriends that beat her up, working at a dead-end job with a kid who despised her. *Most of the time.* Selena waved. "See you later."

Her mom wiggled her fingers on the sofa and nodded. Selena supposed the television show she was watching was quite important. *Life or death.* Every time her friend Alida left the house, her parents asked her where she was going, who she was going with, and when she was coming back. Selena had witnessed the line of questioning on numerous occasions.

Selena couldn't remember a single time anybody had given a shit about her whereabouts.

She shut the door behind her and locked it. She tucked the key in her jeans and headed down the street toward Starbucks. It was dark out, so she was vigilant. Rules of walking alone: No eye contact. Be aware of your surroundings. Keep keys accessible to gouge out eyes, if needed.

As she approached the coffee shop, her stomach went all aflutter. It hit her that she was going on a date with a college guy who was hot and had his own apartment. He was definitely someone worthy of her precious free time. He was someone who had plans and goals, he was going somewhere in this world. A perfect match for her. He wasn't some drunken loser like Fox.

She opened the door to the coffee shop and it jingled the usual tune. She stepped in and spotted Zeek sitting at a table. He had obviously been watching the door since he stood up as soon as she'd entered. He hurried over to her. "Hi. I'm so glad that you were able to make it."

She smiled nervously. "Yeah, well, I was planning to be here anyway."

It wasn't true, but he didn't know that. She even had to change her shift at work so that she could meet up with Zeek. *Zeek.* What kind of name was that? It sounded cool and sophisticated. She liked it.

He said, "Well then, I suppose it's my lucky night. Shall we?" He ushered her over to the register and told the barista, "Hello. I'll have a cappuccino, and what would you like?"

It was definitely a date. He was buying her a drink. Selena wondered if she should order something more grown-up than her usual. *Nah.* She said, "I'll have a Pumpkin Spice Frappuccino." It was fifty degrees outside, but she didn't care. It was her favorite and it was only around for a limited time. She had to get her fix when she could.

After paying, Zeek ushered her over to a table in the corner. Her nerves continued to rattle as she sat down. She hoped she didn't look nervous. That would be too embarrassing.

Zeek dusted off the crumbs on the table onto the floor and then sat down. He stared at her intently. "You look beautiful tonight. I like the way you have your hair. You're like a goddess, all you need is a golden crown and the look would be complete."

Her cheeks burned. "Thank you."

She didn't know what to talk to him about. College? She usually kept her head down and avoided contact with the opposite sex, but there was something about Zeek. Something different, yet familiar.

"Did you have school today?" she asked.

"Yep. I had econ and a few of my computer science classes. Econ is super boring, but I love comp sci. I'm minoring in business too, that's why I have to take econ. I'd like to start my own business one day."

So ambitious. I love that. "What kind of business do you want to start?"

"Something in technology. I don't know, maybe in marketing for a tech company or a tech startup. I really like tech. I write my own software code, but I don't want to be a coder. I'd rather be on the business side in management. I feel like my destiny is to be a CEO. I'm majoring in computer science so that I can understand the products I'll oversee."

Selena watched him intently. "That's so cool." No guys in high school ever talked about wanting to go into business management or becoming a CEO. Most of her female classmates dated stupid jocks or guys who thought they were too cool for school and preferred drinking and drugs to studying or planning for the future. None of them were like Zeek. He clearly had a plan.

He said, "How about you? What are your plans after graduation?"

"I really like my psychology classes, but I also like chemistry and biology, so I was thinking maybe I would go in as a science major. Maybe biology and then maybe become a doctor or a nurse or a psychiatrist. I want to be able to help people, you know?"

She also wanted to make a lot of money and never have to live in a dumpy apartment ever again. She didn't want to worry about how the rent was being paid or how she would procure her next meal. She wanted to be secure physically, mentally, and financially.

"That's great that you know what you want to do at such a young age."

Such a young age? How much older was he? "I've been thinking about it a lot lately since I'm having to apply for schools next month. What year in school are you?"

He sat back. "Well, my third year, but I'm a little bit older because I took time off after high school to backpack through Europe. I just turned twenty-two."

Twenty-two? She never dated anybody that old before. That must be why he was so mature and different than the other guys.

Both of them instinctively turned their head toward the counter after the barista called out their order. He said, "I'll get it."

Selena felt like she had somehow found the one diamond in the dark and dreary cave that was Grapton Hill, California. She couldn't believe she had blown him off the first time they'd met. He was the kind of guy she'd only dreamed about. He was a little older, but it was fine, she'd be eighteen before she knew it. Plus, she was mature for her age, everybody always told her so. It was perfectly logical that she'd date someone older. Why hadn't she figured this out before?

He returned with their drinks and for the next hour, she sipped and watched him as he talked about his future aspirations, hopes for his first job out of college, and maybe one day settling down and having a family. It was so refreshing and inspiring.

She slurped the last bit of her drink. Zeek almost immediately asked her to dinner. She accepted, and they walked a few doors down to the local pizza place. He held the door for her and she walked in and inhaled the scent of baked bread and tomato sauce. She'd thought she'd stepped into heaven. The restaurant itself was rather large, but only a few patrons were sitting around the picnic-style tables. At the counter, they ordered a cheese pizza to share and Zeek ordered a beer.

Seated at the table, he sipped his beer and said, "My god, you're even more beautiful in this light. How do you do it?"

"Just luck, I guess." He'd been complimenting her all night. Selena didn't object. It made her feel special and desired.

"You want a sip?"

She scrunched up her face. "No thanks. I'm not into beer." *Or any alcohol.*

"That's cool. So tell me something about you that nobody knows."

Something nobody knows that was appropriate for a first date? "I hate mushrooms."

He threw his head back and laughed. "Wow! Don't tell me all of your deep dark secrets at once. You'll scare me away." He winked at her.

"You tell me something nobody else knows."

He glanced up to the right. "Hmmm." Before he could answer, the server set down their cheese pizza. He said, "This looks delish. I'm starving." He grabbed a slice and plopped it on his plate. Selena supposed she wouldn't be hearing about any of his dark secrets tonight.

After finishing off the entire pizza, Selena checked the time on her phone and said, "It's almost eleven. I should probably get going. I have school tomorrow morning."

He wiped his mouth with a napkin. "I don't want to keep you out too late. School is the most important thing. Do you want a ride home?"

How did he know she didn't have a car? He must've seen her walk to the Starbucks. "Sure, that would be great." *What a gentlemen.*

As they exited the restaurant, he reached for her hand and she let him take it into his. They were holding hands. On a first date. Was that cheesy or romantic? The jolt of electricity racing through her body screamed *romantic*. Was she falling for him already? She wondered how he felt about her. She didn't want to be one of those girls who hounded him with stupid questions like, "What are you thinking?" or "How do you feel about me?" No, she'd play it cool. He opened the car door for her and she slid into his new Honda Civic. It still had that new car smell.

She was excited to be dating a guy with a car, a nice car, not some POS. He started the engine and heavy metal blasted through the speakers. He turned it down and said, "I'm so sorry. I like to rock out."

With a reassuring smile she said, " It's cool." She sat with her hands in her lap as she watched him drive the half mile down the street to her apartment building.

As they drove she wondered if he'd judge her based on where she lived. It was a dump. There was no other way to describe it. She now knew he was from a good family with a mom and a dad and a brother and a sister. And he was dropping her off at the shit hole that was barely habitable. She wondered if he'd break it off with her after he saw where she lived. She hoped not. She said, "This is me right here."

He parked the car and she exited the vehicle. He hopped out

and insisted on walking her to the door. *And here I thought chivalry was an urban legend.*

At the door, he said, "I had a wonderful time with you. I hope you let me see you again."

She gazed up at him and grinned. "I had a good time too. Of course you can see me again."

He cupped her cheeks in his hands and kissed her lightly on the mouth. Electricity buzzed through her. She thought, *And he's a good kisser.*

He stepped back. "Have a good night. Dream of me, because I'll definitely be dreaming of you."

She waved. It was a little corny, but kinda sweet too. She opened the door and tried to hide her obvious happiness from her mother. She shut the door behind her and waved to her mother, still on the living room sofa watching television, and hustled back to her bedroom.

Nestled in the privacy of her room, she smiled and gleefully screamed into her pillow. Tonight, she'd had the best first date of her life. Things were looking up. A few minutes later, the buzz of her phone pulled her away from the pillow. It was a text from Zeek.

HI BEAUTIFUL. I HAD A GREAT TIME TONIGHT. MISSING YOU ALREADY.

Laying on her stomach, she texted back. ME TOO.

WHAT ARE YOU WEARING?

SAME OUTFIT AS TEN MINUTES AGO.

TEASE ME.

She shook her head. *Uh-huh. Not so fast.* She texted. GOODNIGHT.

XOXO.

She put away her phone, changed into her flannel pajamas, and crashed on her bed, very much hoping to have dreams filled with Zeek and his soft lips.

5

Selena sat across from Alida at lunch. "How did you do on the test?"

Alida pulled back her dark curly hair and tucked it behind her ear. "I did okay. Maybe B plus or A minus. How about you?"

Selena had been going out with Zeek every free night she had. She couldn't help it, she had a new addiction to add to her Pumpkin Spice Frappuccinos and his name was Zeek. He made her feel beautiful and special and loved. It was the best feeling in the world. But dating him did mean she had less study time, and she feared she hadn't done very well on the exam. "That's cool. Not sure I did so hot, but we'll see."

"I wouldn't worry, I'm sure you did fine. Enough about boring old chem. How are things with the new boyfriend?"

"Things are great."

Selena glanced at her phone. Another text from Zeek popped up on her screen. She loved how he texted her all day, every day. It was so sweet.

Alida said, "Zeek again?"

Selena nodded. "Yeah, he's so sweet. And so hot."

Alida smirked. "Well he certainly likes to text a lot. I don't know if I've seen you in the last three weeks when you weren't feverishly texting him."

"It's what you do when you're in a relationship. I think it's because he's older. Older guys are better at communication than high school boys."

Alida seemed skeptical, but Selena shrugged it off.

"Well, I hope he's not taking too much of your time. How are your college applications going?"

Selena looked away. She hadn't started. The deadline was in two weeks. Maybe she should tell Zeek that she needed to cut back their time together? She wasn't doing a good job managing all of the things that she needed to get done. Maybe they needed to take a mini break. She was sure he'd understand. He knew that she was college-bound and had goals and aspirations. Just like him. She would talk to him about it. She was sure he'd be supportive, but it would kill her to be away from him for too long. She finally said, "I haven't really started, but I plan to work on them on Saturday. I already know what I'm going to write about in my essays, I just need to do the first draft this weekend and then revise the week after that. It'll be fine."

Alida shook her head. "You're so much more calm than I would be. If I didn't already have my apps in, I'd be freaking the freak out. But I've always been more cautious than you."

Was that true? Selena always thought she had played it safe. No drinking. No drugs. Good grades. Part-time job. Why would Alida say such a thing?

6

Blindfolded, Selena walked stiffly with her arms stretched out in front of her as Zeek led her by the hand to the center of his one-bedroom apartment. After dinner, when he'd first asked if she would wear a bandana over her eyes, because he had a surprise for her, she was apprehensive. She wasn't sure where they were going, but she recognized the need to go up one flight of stairs and turn immediately to the right. They were going to his apartment.

He took off her blindfold and her mouth dropped open. There had to be twenty glittering candles throughout the space. A bouquet of fragrant red roses sat on the coffee table next to a tiny box with a red bow on top. A jewelry box. For her? She beamed at him. "What is all this?"

He grabbed her by the waist and said, "Happy one-month anniversary."

He remembered. "Happy one-month anniversary to you too."

He kissed her fiercely and her body temperature rose. They still hadn't gone all the way. She wanted to wait, mostly because she was terrified of getting pregnant and turning into her mother. Debbie had been telling Selena since she could remember that if she hadn't gotten pregnant with Selena at eighteen, she would've had a much better life. *Noted. Thanks, Mom.* Selena vowed to not turn out like her. Zeek had been so sweet and so understanding. He hadn't pushed her to do anything she wasn't comfortable with.

He stepped back and led her over to his navy blue futon. He sat her down and faced her. "There is something I've been wanting to tell you." He seemed to stare into her soul. "Babe, I love you."

Selena grinned. "I love you too."

Zeek responded with glee in his eyes. They were like a blue sky full of shining stars. He said, "I have something for you."

He picked up the white ring-sized box with a little red metallic bow on top and handed it to her.

She was shocked. And delighted. She'd never been given a piece of jewelry before. Not that she'd had any boyfriends, she'd tried to stay away from the opposite sex, fearful of making the mistakes of her mother. Selena assumed she paused too long when he said with excitement in his voice, "Come on, open it."

She took the top off and turned the box over. A gray velvet ring box sat in her hand. She popped it open and gasped. It was a gold ring with five little diamonds in the shape of a heart. She was so stunned she couldn't even look at him. Her eyes fixated on the ring.

"Well, do you like it?"

"Yes, it's beautiful. Thank you." Was it a ring with meaning? She didn't know. She didn't think he was proposing to her. *That would be insane, right?*

"It's a promise ring. This may sound nuts, but I know in my heart that I will marry you one day. Obviously not right now, but one day after we're both done with school. This ring is a promise that one day I will marry you. Will you accept this promise?"

He wanted to marry her one day? Sure, she'd fantasized about herself in a white dress and him in a black suit someday far, far off into the future. She was head over heels in love with him. How could she not fantasize about the future? But here he was making a commitment *now*, years in advance of the actual event. It was charming and romantic and more than she could have ever hoped for. She was so grateful that he had walked into her life. She scrunched up into her shoulders and said, "Yes, I accept this promise."

Zeek grinned from ear to ear, before pulling her close. "Perfect. That makes me so happy. Plus, this way everyone will know you belong to me."

Belong to him? Was that sweet or controlling? She shook herself. *Stop over-thinking it, Selena. He loves you. Enjoy it.*

He kissed her passionately, gently pushing her back down onto the futon. She didn't stop him. Her body was on fire. She was ready. She was ready to give herself to him. How lucky was she to have her first time be with the love of her life, the man she would one day marry?

Laying next to Zeek on the futon with her arm draped across his chest, Selena gazed up at him. "I love you so much, Zeek."

"I love you too, babe." They shared a soft kiss and then he said, "Stay the night. Please. I can't imagine anything better than waking up with you in my arms. It would be like a dream come true. I love you so much it hurts. I can't believe I have been so lucky to find you. My soulmate. The woman I'll spend the rest of my life with. It's a great love, one for the ages. Don't you agree?"

"Yes, but I can't, you know that." She would love to sleep in his arms all night and wake up next to him. His face being the first thing she saw. But she had school the next day. As it was, she'd only finished her Cal State University applications. She still had the UC's to fill out. The deadline was only two days away. She needed to put the finishing touches on her essays before hitting submit on the applications. She still hadn't had a conversation with Zeek about maybe spending a little bit less time together so that she could study more for school. She didn't have a parent who questioned why her grades were slipping, but she herself feared the repercussions. She knew she needed to focus more on school. It was important she get her grades back up, especially with finals coming up. She would have to have the conversation with Zeek pretty soon. But not tonight. The night was too magical to ruin with such practicalities.

She pushed open the door to her apartment, trying to be as quiet as she could. It was nearly one in the morning. Mom was likely in bed, but Selena wasn't positive that was the case. She eased in and was delighted to see that her mom wasn't in the living room.

A perfect ending to a perfect night. She was on cloud nine. She'd never been so happy in her whole life, and soon she'd be eighteen and off to college. She still couldn't fathom that she'd landed the most wonderful, amazing, smart, and talented boyfriend who would one day be her husband. How did she get so lucky? She just had to endure six more months with Debbie and then she would be free.

She tiptoed through the living room, careful not to wake her mother. Her face fell and then her body froze. A pair of men's boots sat next to the sofa. Fox's boots. He was in the apartment.

Selena shook herself out her trance and hurried quietly to her room, trying to be as silent as she possibly could. Heart pounding, she made it her bedroom and closed the door softly behind her. How could her mom let that violent attempted-murderer back in their home? Did her mother want to die? Terror filled every cell in Selena's body. What if he came after her too?

7

Selena was jolted from her thoughts by the creaking of her mother's bed on the other side of their shared wall. Panic shot through her and she couldn't think straight. She needed to get out of there, and fast. She grabbed her backpack and shoved in her books, notes, and some clothes that were strewn about on her bed.

Footsteps in the hall.

She darted over to the window. Noise be damned, she slid open the window.

Her doorknob jangled.

She turned to look and her eyes met Fox's evil stare, narrowed on her. She hurled her backpack and herself over the windowsill and ran.

Sweat dripped down her back as her heart practically jumped out of her chest. She didn't stop until she reached the Starbucks. She scurried to hide behind the building and out of plain site. She didn't think Fox was following her, but she wasn't sure. Would he come looking for her? She didn't know. She pulled her phone from her backpack and texted Zeek.

CAN YOU PICK ME UP?

She waited what seemed like an eternity, but in all likelihood it was only a few seconds.

WHY WHAT'S WRONG?

FOX IS BACK.

WHERE ARE YOU?

BEHIND STARBUCKS.

I'M NOT FAR. BE THERE SOON. XOXO

She shivered, partially due to the cold and partially due to fear. Had Fox been waiting for her? What would've happened had she not been with Zeek that night?

Every awful scenario flooded through her mind. Guys like Fox did all types of horrible things, she was sure of it. After what he'd done to her mom last time, she just couldn't believe her mother would let him back in. Had her mother given up on her own life? Given up on Selena's? Did she not see that not only was she endangering her life, but Selena's too? Tears flowed freely down her face. She could taste the salty tears in her mouth. *Gross.* She wiped her cheeks and mouth with the sleeves of her sweatshirt.

Headlights swung across the parking lot.

She peeked around the wall. Relief washed over her. She sprinted over to Zeek's car and opened the passenger side door and slid in, throwing her backpack on the floor. She flung her arms around Zeek and cried.

———

Back at Zeek's apartment, she told him everything that had happened, including the full details of her mother's first attack by Fox. Her mom had almost died. Now Fox was back. Why? To finish the job?

She had been too ashamed to tell Zeek before that she had a mother who would allow a man do that to her, let alone allow him back in their home. She despised her mother most of the time, but she did love her. This was her mom. Her only family. What would happen if ... what if it already happened?

With Zeek up to speed, she asked him, "Should I call the police? What if my mom is hurt?"

"Did she tell the police it was Fox who attacked her the first time?"

Selena shook her head. "No, but I know it was him."

"Why don't we give it some time? Your mom is probably okay. Let's get a good night's sleep. I'll take you back over there tomorrow to get some of your things. I don't want you going over there alone. You can stay here as long as you like. I don't know what I would do if I lost you."

Selena hugged him. "Okay." He really was her knight in shining armor. The hero in her fucked-up un-fairytale of a life.

After dinner the next day, Zeek drove Selena over to her apartment. She'd skipped school that day and called in sick to work. She needed a day to collect herself and put together a plan. She'd always been a planner; now she needed a new plan. A plan to stay safe and alive.

Thank God she had Zeek to help her. She put her key into her apartment's lock and pushed the door open. Zeek put his arm across the door and said, "No, let me go in first. We don't know if he's still in there."

Selena nodded.

Zeek pushed open the door and Selena followed behind. He continued to the living room. Selena didn't see any sign of Fox's boots. She followed Zeek but stopped at that unmistakable smell. *No. Not again.* Selena called out, "Mom?"

No response.

Zeek turned around and said, "What's that smell?"

Selena felt the blood rush out of her body. "We ... We should check my mom's bedroom."

Zeek grabbed her hand and continued down the hallway. The smell got stronger. Selena covered her mouth to block the scent of urine and feces. And something else. A vile new scent added to the mix.

Her mother's bedroom door was ajar. Zeek continued slowly and stopped before Selena could enter. He mumbled, "Oh my God."

"What is it, how is she?"

Deep down, Selena knew exactly how her mother was. But she didn't *know* know. She needed to know. She continued in and stopped in the middle of her mother's bedroom. Selena stared down at the bed. The contents of her stomach were approaching fast. She rushed to the hallway bathroom and vomited in the toilet. Holding the rim, she shook her head.

He'd done it. He'd killed her.

8

Selena stared blankly out the kitchen window. Zeek had his arm around her shoulders in what she assumed was an attempt to comfort her. It wasn't working. How could it? She was sitting across the table from a homicide detective who was asking her about what had happened to her mother. She explained she had just stopped by to pick up a few things and they found her like that.

"Ms. Bailey?"

"What?" She refocused on the police officer. He was old, with gray hair and vacant eyes, like a disinterested grandpa. No doubt he'd seen this sort of thing before.

"When was the last time you were here?"

She fixed her gaze on the window that overlooked their small patio. It was mostly filled with junk and dead plants from that time her mother tried to get sober. That had lasted less than a week. "Last night, I guess it was this morning, around one o'clock in the morning. I came in through the front door ..." Should she tell him about Fox? He knew she'd seen him here. What if Fox came after her in retaliation?

Was this her fault? Should she have forced her mom to tell the police it had been Fox who had almost killed her a month ago? Why hadn't Selena told the police? Would it have stopped him from killing her mom? Why hadn't she done more? She had been so focused on getting the hell out of the place that she didn't think about what it would really be like if she lost her mom.

"What did you notice, Ms. Bailey?"

It was time to be brave. "I saw a pair of men's boots in our living room. They were Fox's boots."

"Who's Fox? Do you know his last name?"

She didn't look at the officer. "He's my mom's, *was* my mom's boyfriend. They'd been dating for the last few months. I'm pretty sure he's the one who attacked her last time. They'd always fight. Always get drunk. I don't know his last name or if Fox is his real name."

"Did you ever see him hit your mom before?"

Selena had always sequestered herself in her bedroom when he was around. She hadn't liked him from day one. "No, but I heard him. We share a bedroom wall and sometimes I heard what sounded like he was pushing her against the wall or slapping her."

"You never called the police?"

Was it her fault? What if she *had* called the police? Her mother had always begged her not to. Fox wasn't the first boyfriend to take his aggression out on Debbie. "No. Mom always told me not to call the police. She said it just made them mad, more mad. Fox wasn't the first to hit her. I kept mostly to myself and tried to avoid her scumbag boyfriends."

"What did you do after you saw his boots?"

She turned to look at the detective. "I hurried to my room and tried not to make any noise. I packed a few things and was about to leave when I heard him open the door. I turned back and saw him and he saw me. I went through the window and ran as fast as I could."

"Where did you go?"

"To the Starbucks down Grapton Avenue, behind the building, and I hid."

Where would she live? How could she avoid foster care? Would it make a difference if she tried to find her dad? That's assuming he was still alive. She didn't even know if he was. For all she knew, she was now an orphan. Darkness descended on her. She didn't want to be an orphan.

"How old are you, Ms. Bailey?"

She looked into the detective's dark brown eyes. "I'm eighteen."

"Do you have a place to stay tonight?"

She turned to Zeek. He squeezed her tight and said, "Of course you can stay with me as long as you need."

"I'll stay with Zeek."

She sensed the police officer was skeptical of her age, but if he was any kind of human being, he wouldn't push her right now. "Can we go?" she asked.

"Yes, let me give you my card. My partner or I will be in touch. Most likely my partner. He's out of town right now, but he'll most likely take over the case when he returns. You may want to gather a few things. The apartment will be a crime scene for a while, and you won't be allowed back in until it's cleared. I'll have one of the officers escort you into your bedroom and you can pack up some things."

She nodded. She glanced around the apartment now swarming with police officers. It was as if it was all happening in slow motion, like a bad dream.

Back at Zeek's apartment, he sat her down on the futon and told her that she could stay as long as she wanted. *Forever, even.* She realized that if it wasn't for Zeek, she'd be homeless or lost in the system. He asked, "Are you sure you're okay?"

"I'll be fine. Probably should try to get some sleep. I have school tomorrow." She wasn't sure she would actually sleep, but she didn't want to talk anymore and didn't have the energy to be upright.

"You plan to go to school tomorrow?"

Her new reality included living with her boyfriend, going to school, going to work. It all happened so fast. She said, "What else would I do? I'd go nuts just sitting around here all day by myself. And I already missed today."

"Okay. I'll drive you to school in the morning."

Driving me to school. Paying my rent. She'd always been independent, and it was how she wanted it to remain. But how could she? Could she increase her hours at work or get a higher - paying job? Would it be enough?

"I can take the bus. It's fine."

"I insist. I will take you to school. It's the least I can do."

"Thank you. I love you."

"I love you too, babe. Anything you need, you just let me know. You know I'm a man who takes care of his girl." He kissed her on the forehead, sat back, and smiled.

His girl. She liked the sound of that.

9

Selena moped down the hallway of her high school toward the cafeteria. She started to wonder if maybe she should have stayed at Zeek's. She didn't think she remembered a single thing anyone said or did in any of her classes that morning. All she could think about was how unimportant everything was. Her mother had just died. Murdered. At the moment, she gave zero fucks about hyperboles and paradoxes. She entered the cafeteria and spotted Alida and her other friends seated at a nearby table. She walked up to Alida. "Hey, can I talk to you for second?"

"Of course."

They found an empty bench and sat down. Alida asked, "What's wrong? Did something happen with you and Zeek? You seemed totally spaced out during English. I've never seen you like this. You know you can talk to me about anything, right?"

Selena nodded. "It's not Zeek. My mom. She. She died."

Alida's mouth dropped open and her hand flung over it. She composed herself and said, "I'm so sorry. What happened?"

"She was killed. I think by Fox. Zeek and I found her last night." Selena looked away.

Alida wrapped her arms around her.

Selena began to sob. Saying it out loud made it more real. Selena sat up and wiped her eyes on the backs of her hands. "Yeah. So, that's why I'm distracted."

"My gosh. How horrifying. I can't even imagine. Wait. Where are you staying? Have they got this guy Fox? Are you safe?"

"Zeek said that I can move in with him. I stayed with him last night and I guess that's where I'll live. He says he loves me and wants to marry me one day. Look at what he gave me." She put out her hand and wiggled her fingers.

But Alida responded with a look of horror. "Are you engaged?!"

"Oh no, it was our one-month anniversary and he gave it to me as a promise ring. He says one day he wants to marry me, but he knows and I know, obviously, that we're both too young and he needs to finish college and I need to go to college, but isn't it sweet?" There was at least one happy thing in her life.

"I mean, that's nice of him, but what about college? What about your applications? Have you finished? What about the senior project? Our written portion is due in two weeks. How well do you even know this guy?"

Selena became agitated. Alida didn't understand what was like to have a real boyfriend. A serious boyfriend who loved her. She said, "I have all my Cal State applications in. The only ones I didn't finish where the UC's because my essays weren't finished. Today is the deadline so I don't see that happening, but the CSU system is fine for me. It's cheaper anyways."

Alida still looked at her as if she was making a horrible mistake. Alida didn't know what was like to have an alcoholic mother and absentee father or to have her mother murdered. Why was she giving her such a hard time? Couldn't she just be supportive? And be happy that she had found someone who loved her?

Alida furrowed her brow. "I can ask my parents if you can stay with us. I'm sure they'll say yes. They really like you and it's only for another semester and then you'll go off to college. I'll ask them tonight when I get home from school, okay?"

Selena shook her head. "Oh no, it's fine. I want to stay with Zeek. It'll be fine."

Selena could tell Alida wasn't buying that she was *fine*. As much as she loved Zeek, it was a little off-plan to move in with a guy at the age of seventeen.

Alida said, "Selena, honey, I love you. You're my best friend. I'm worried about you. I think you're a lot better off staying with me and my family. I'll talk to my parents tonight."

"You don't have to worry about me. Really. I just wanted to tell you because you should know, but I'm fine. Really. I'll be fine. Now let's go join the others for lunch." Selena would be fine. She was a survivor. This is was just one more bump in her crappy road to a better life, right?

"Are you going to buy lunch?"

"Not really hungry." She wasn't.

Alida eyed her and then said, "Okay."

Alida and Selena rejoined the group at the table. Selena slid onto the metal bench. She tried to force a smile at the other girls talking about nail polish. A conversation that under normal circumstances she'd be into. Makeup. Nail polish. Hairstyles. Clothes. She'd loved talking over those things and imagining styles based on what her friends were describing. But now the only thing she could see was her mother's eyes. The dim light that used to be there had been fully extinguished.

Selena's phone buzzed on the metal table and she looked at the screen. She didn't know the number. It was local. She answered, "Hello?"

"Is this Selena Bailey?"

"Yes."

"This is Detective Renier. We met yesterday."

Selena climbed out from the bench and walked to a quieter place in the corner of the bustling cafeteria. "Yeah, I remember."

"We were wondering if you would be able to come to the station to give us more information about what happened yesterday. Do you think you could come down here after school?"

Selena shrugged to nobody at all. "Yeah, I can probably get a ride from Zeek."

"My partner could pick you up, if that makes it easier?"

Selena gave it some thought. She didn't want to be seen having a cop car pick her up from school. Did detectives drive around in regular cop cars? On TV shows they didn't. She didn't really want to be seen having two old guys picking her up from school either.

"Maybe you could pick me up across the street from school at the Chevron."

"Okay, Ms. Bailey, we'll see you at three o'clock at Chevron."

She ended the call and headed back over to the table with the rest of her friends.

One teased, "Was that the boyfriend? Oh my gosh, you have to tell us all the details! Alida says he gave you a promise ring. That's so romantic. I'm totes jelly."

She forced a smile and told them the details of their romantic one-month anniversary celebration, but obviously she left out the parts about how she'd spent the night after fleeing her apartment and finding her mother's dead body the next day.

After school Selena waited across the street at the gas station. A black sedan pulled up. She saw Detective Renier in the driver seat and a much younger man, presumably a detective, in the passenger seat. Detective Renier rolled down the window and said, "Hi, Selena. This is my partner, Detective Gates. Go ahead and hop in the back."

She nodded and waved hello to the younger detective. She slid into the back of the car and put her backpack on the seat next to her. She wrinkled her nose at the scent of stale cigarettes, but otherwise it seemed like just a normal car.

They drove in silence to the station. Once they arrived, the detectives escorted her to their office area. There were desks everywhere. It looked like a call center on TV, where people were busy trying to sell you some stupid thing over the phone. *Very retro.* She realized this was the first time she'd been in a police station. It was surprising that she had never been inside one before.

She sat down in a chair next to Detective Renier's desk. Detective Gates pulled up a chair. The two detectives faced her. The young detective had bright blue eyes and dark hair. He was kinda cute for an older guy. He said, "Like Detective Renier mentioned, I'm his partner, Detective Gates, and I'll be taking over the investigation of your mother's death. I know that you gave us a statement yesterday, but I was hoping to get a bit more information about Fox. I'll need you to tell me everything that you know about him."

Selena let out a breath. "I don't know much. He was a jerk. He drank a lot. He never had a smile on his face. I stayed away from him. I don't know his last name. I think my mom met him at one of the bars she goes to—went to—a lot. I think it's called the Roundup and Inn or something like that. There's a motel attached."

The detective scribbled on a notepad. "You said the Roundup and Inn, is that like I-N, or like a hotel, I-N-N?"

"I-N-N like a hotel."

"Okay, that's really helpful. So far we haven't been able to find Fox, but we're still processing the scene. Hopefully fingerprints will help us catch the person who did this. Can you give us a description of what Fox looks like? It may be helpful to have you sit with a sketch artist. Would you be able to do that for us, Selena?"

She looked over her shoulder at a few officers standing in a nearby corner. There was a lot going on. A lot of crime.

"Selena?"

"Sorry. Yeah, I could give you a description."

"Great, we'll bring down the sketch artist." Detective Gates nodded at Detective Renier. "Do you want to go get the artist? I'll ask Selena here a few more questions while we're waiting."

Detective Renier pushed himself off his chair with the assistance of his desk. The old guy wasn't in shape. This was who was supposed to be fighting the bad guys? He said, "Aye, aye. Captain." And trotted off.

Detective Gates lowered his voice. "You're not eighteen, are you?"

She shook her head. He wouldn't be asking unless he already knew. She had always been told she looked young for her age too. It always irked her, now more than ever.

"Where are you staying? It says here that you're staying with a Zeek Tate. Is that correct?"

"Yeah."

"There's nobody else you can stay with?"

She didn't think so. Maybe Alida's family, but she had a feeling Alida was more optimistic than she should be. Sure, her family liked Selena, but were they willing to take on a teenage orphan? "Not really. A friend said she could check with her parents, but so far nobody else."

"Do you know where your father is?"

She shook her head. "He left us a long time ago and I haven't seen him. Uh, it's probably been five, six years. He's an addict."

"No other family—grandparents, aunts, uncles, no one?"

"Not that I know of. I'm sure I have grandparents some-where, but my mom wasn't in touch with them. I only have vague memories from when I was little. I don't get Christmas cards or anything."

The detective seemed to be pained by her story. That was nice of him.

"I understand you're a senior in high school. What are your plans for after graduation?"

"College. I've already applied to five Cal State universities. I should get in somewhere, I think. I have pretty good grades." At least, she had up until recently.

Detective Gates nodded. "Okay, here's what I'm gonna do. You seem like a good kid. Sounds like you've got plans for school and for your future. Between you and me, staying with a friend is probably better than with a boyfriend, but even with a boyfriend is probably better than putting you in the system. You're close to eighteen, hopefully it won't get flagged. But, let me ask you this, how well do you know this Zeek Tate? How long have you been together?"

"We've been dating for a little over a month. He's from Ridgemont and he is a student at Cal State East Bay. He's really smart."

"How did you meet?"

"At Starbucks. It's like my favorite place. It's my home away from home when I don't want to be at home, which is most of the time because of my mom and all her boyfriends ..." Her train of thought shifted. Her mom was gone. She stared down at the ground.

"I know this is tough. It sounds like you were dealt a bad hand. And for that I'm sorry. I'm sorry for your loss and for your situation. I want us to keep in close contact until we catch Fox. He knows you saw him, and if he's the one who did this, he may come after you. I'll call you and check up on you daily. I'll also give you my business card so you can call if something spooks you or you have any questions. Is that okay, at least until I can ensure your safety?"

She nodded, keeping her gaze on the floor. Her nose began to tingle. She sniffled and tried to blink the tears away. She had to be strong.

The detective handed her a tissue he'd plucked from atop his desk, she accepted it and dabbed her eyes. She sat there in silence, she wasn't sure for how long. The detective didn't leave or try to console her.

In a soothing voice he said, "The sketch artist is here for you. Are you ready?"

She looked at him. "I'm ready."

"This won't take too long. Afterward I can take you home, okay?"

She nodded. "Thanks."

He gave her a warm smile. In that smile, Selena could tell Detective Gates was a good man. Why weren't there more of them?

10

Selena reached the door to Zeek's apartment and waved goodbye to the detective. She turned around and stood face to face with Zeek. His face was red and his eyes wide. "Who the hell was that?"

His tone was accusatory. She'd texted him from the police station, so why was he acting surprised that the detective had dropped her off? "That was Detective Gates. I told you he was driving me home."

"That wasn't the detective from yesterday. So who was it?"

Selena shook her head. Trying to keep an even tone, she explained again. "That was Detective Gates, Detective Renier's partner. Detective Renier was that old guy we talked to yesterday. Detective Gates is taking over the investigation, like Detective Renier said yesterday. I don't understand why you're so upset."

"Why didn't you tell me that he was young? Are you attracted to him?"

Selena was shocked. What had happened to her sweet, loving boyfriend? She watched as his eye twitched. She thought that if he had special powers, he would've burned a hole right through her. She said, "Of course not. He literally just drove me home. I love you so much. I would never even look at another guy."

She put her arms up, hoping to give him a hug, but his chest was puffed out and his body rigid. She pleaded, "Zeek, you're my whole world. Why would I be interested in some old guy? He has to be at least thirty. Zeek, come on. I love you. You know that."

Zeek's body relaxed and he put his hands around her waist. He bowed his head. "You mean it? You love me and only me?"

Selena brushed his hair from his brow. "Of course, Zeek. I love you so much."

"I just don't know what I would do without you. I love you so much. Thinking of you with another guy makes me crazy."

She smiled sweetly at him. "You never have to worry about me with another guy."

They embraced and he kissed her passionately. She never had a boyfriend who got jealous. It was sweet. No one had ever loved her so passionately before. It made her inside glow. She felt like the luckiest girl in the world.

They sat down at the dining table. She grinned across it at him. "How was your day?" She chuckled. "Is that so weird to ask? It's something an old married couple would say."

Zeek's face returned to its normal color and his eyes shined at her. "I like it. I like you here. My day was okay. I went to class and then worked in the computer lab for a while. How about you?"

"Well, going to school was maybe not the best idea. I couldn't really concentrate. All of it seemed so meaningless. But I was thinking about the future, and I'm going to talk to my boss about increasing my hours so I can help out around here. I don't want you to have to support me. I'll help pay for rent and utilities."

"You don't have to do that. I can take care of you. My rent is paid for by my parents, plus I have a job. You don't have to worry about any of this. Actually, if you wanted you could even quit your job."

She'd never quit her job. Not for a man, even the man she loved. She'd always been independent. She didn't want to lean on anyone for anything. That much she knew. She said, "Oh no, I'm keeping my job. I'll keep the same hours for now, that way I'll have some spending money and I can still save for college." *What would he do, put me on an allowance like a kept woman? Does he not understand me at all?*

He put his arms across the small bistro table, indicating he wanted Selena to put her hands in his. She did and he said, "If that's what you want, it's fine, but I'm more than capable of taking care of you and nothing would make me happier."

She grinned. It was so sweet and such a loving gesture. She couldn't imagine a life where all she had to do was go to school like a normal teenager. Not that she'd ever be a normal teenager, but the idea of someone taking care of her for a change was awfully nice.

A few days later, Selena stood in the living room with her phone pressed to her ear. She laughed. "Okay, thanks, Detective Gates." She hung up the phone and looked up at Zeek. That look had returned to his eyes. That accusatory look.

He scowled. "The detective again?"

"Yes, he was giving me an update on the case. They got a hit on a set of fingerprints at the scene. They think they're Fox's. Detective Gates has an arrest warrant and is going to pick him up tonight. It's great news."

"Sure, but why does he keep calling you? He's called every

single day. More than once a day sometimes. I don't get it, you sure there isn't something going on?"

She didn't know how to deal with Zeek when he was like this. How could she get him to understand? "No, the detective told me on Tuesday that until they caught Fox he wanted to keep an eye on me to make sure I was safe. He was worried that Fox would come after me, so he checks in on me, lets me know what's going on with the case."

"He doesn't need to protect you. You have me. You can tell him to stop calling."

Selena didn't know what to say. He was a police detective trying to solve the murder of her mother and she was a witness in the case. Why did Zeek keep thinking it was something else? It was starting to get on her nerves. Did he not trust her?

She said, "He needs to keep me apprised of the case. Once they bring Fox in, he said I'll need to pick him out of a lineup. I think this is all very normal."

"Normal? Normal that some guy has been calling my girlfriend twice a day for the last three days? I think he's into you."

She shook her head. "I don't think so. I think that's crazy."

Zeek began pacing the length of the apartment. He raised his voice. "Are you calling me crazy? I'm not crazy. You're beautiful and gorgeous and young. I'm sure he's lusting after you every night. Why can't you see that? Don't you know how guys think? I'm a guy and I know. I bet he's jerking off to you right now."

Selena recoiled. Zeek had never been so vulgar before. It wasn't attractive. She didn't think the detective was pleasuring himself to thoughts of her. Where did he get these weird ideas from?

"What, you have nothing to say to that? Because you know it's true! That's why he calls you, to hear your sweet young voice. Oh yeah, I'm sure he fantasizes about you. His story about protecting you is his way of getting close to you. I can protect you. I'm here all the time with you. I will protect you. Not him," Zeek fumed.

Selena didn't think she could win this argument or talk any sense into him. She would just let it play out and hoped he tired of this jealous routine. At first it was sweet, but now it was turning her off, big time. She sighed. Nobody was perfect. If this was Zeek's one imperfection, she supposed that wasn't too bad.

"What, no response?"

"Well, he's a detective."

"So you think he's tougher than I am? Is that what you're saying?" He stood in front of her, hands on his hips.

She imagined steam coming out of his ears. He was so worked up. It was strange and kind of scary. He shouted. "Answer me, do you think he's tougher than I am?"

She moved away from him. "No, of course not. But please calm down. You're starting to scare me."

He put both hands on the arms of her chair and hovered over her. "Don't ever tell me what to do. Never tell me what to do."

A ripple of fear ran through her. Had Alida been right? How well did she really know Zeek? Selena couldn't look at him. She averted her gaze and stared at the beige carpet.

He pushed off her chair and continued pacing the apartment, huffing and puffing.

Selena just did not understand. Why was he so mad? Why had she not seen him fly off into a rage before she had moved in? She'd had this feeling in her gut before. The feeling when she'd hear one of her mother's boyfriend slap her or push her against the wall. *That's crazy. Zeek isn't like that.* Mom's boyfriends were never loving or caring or ever bought her any jewelry. This wasn't the same. This was different. Zeek loved her. He was just having a hard time. Maybe he was stressed out. He saw a dead body too, she reminded herself. Maybe she needed to be more understanding. She didn't know what it was like to have the life of a college student. But how could it be more stressful than her life? Maybe something else was going on with them that she didn't know about. Maybe she should ask him once he calmed down. Maybe he was having a difficult time at school or work.

She remained frozen in the chair at the dining table. He was coming toward her again with a long look on his face. The rage seemed to have seeped out of him and been replaced with sadness. He knelt on the ground and buried his face in her lap, his hands around her waist. "I'm so sorry I overreacted. I have a lot of my mind. I love you. You're so beautiful, I just always think, what man wouldn't want you? I love you so much." He lifted his head and said, "Please forgive me. I need you." He stood up. "Come with me." He gave her his hand and she took it.

Apprehensively she followed him over to the futon. He sat her down and then pushed her back. Her heart was beating fast. She wasn't sure if she should be scared or turned on. He said, "I need you so bad. Make love to me. Make love to me, say you will."

She wasn't exactly in the mood. "Of course. I love you too."

He kissed her roughly and she struggled to get air. She didn't like how aggressive he was being. He grabbed her breasts and tugged hard, ignoring her muffled cry. He unbuttoned her jeans and shoved them down to her ankles with his foot. He unbuttoned his pants and pushed his jeans and boxers down before he jammed himself inside of her. She yelped quietly.

He said, "Oh, that's so good. Oh. Yes. You like that, don't you."

She nodded as he rammed his tongue in her mouth. When he finished, about thirty seconds later, he kissed her on the cheek. His sweat stuck to her skin. She tried not to flinch or turn away. He mumbled. "Babe, I love you so much. That was so good."

She couldn't look at him. It wasn't anything like the few times they'd done it before. He had been patient and giving. This was something entirely different. *Thank god I decided to start taking the pill right after we started dating. What the hell?*

He climbed off her and headed into the bathroom. She heard the shower turn on. She wondered, did he think that was making love? Maybe that was how he liked it? She supposed that when you loved someone, sometimes you had to do what they want, even if you didn't like it. She loved him and he loved her, and that was all that mattered, right?

11

Selena sat at the kitchen table reading her pre-calculus textbook. It wasn't making any sense. Maybe she was too distracted for homework. She was scheduled to go down to the police station to try to pick out Fox from a lineup. It was also the one-week mark of her mother's death. It seemed so long ago, yet like it had only been five minutes. How could seven days change so much? Her mom was dead. She'd moved in with her new boyfriend. Finals were right around the corner, and she needed to concentrate. She read the problem again. Maybe she should just try later. She heard the sound of the front door open and close. She smiled. It was her favorite part of the day. Zeek called out, "Honey, I'm home."

It had become their little joke, a throwback to the 1950s. He walked up to her and gave her a kiss on the cheek. "What are you studying? Pre-calculus?"

"Yeah, I keep reading this one problem over and over again. I'm just not in the right headspace."

He said, "Maybe I can help. I told you that I basically aced all the math classes I've ever taken since I was like four, right?"

Four-year-olds don't typically take math class, but if you want to show off what a great, mathematician you are, be my guest. Selena bit back her snarky thought. She supposed she shouldn't get annoyed with him. Zeek was not only hot, but also kind of a nerd. It was such a turn-on.

"I don't know, I don't think I can concentrate right now."

He leaned over and studied the page. "Oh, it's simple. Don't feel bad. Girls aren't good at math, not like guys."

Girls aren't good at math? Selena seethed silently. She wanted to scream that she actually had an A in her pre-calculus class and it usually came pretty easily to her. She was just under pressure right now and having a hard time concentrating. She shook her head. "No, it's not that I don't understand math. I'm just distracted right now."

"If you say so. When do we need to leave for the police station?"

If I say so? Jesus. Was she dating a misogynist? *Whatever.* "We should leave in ten minutes, Detective Gates asked that I be there at five."

She watched as Zeek's demeanor went rigid and then back to relaxed. Zeek still wasn't thrilled the detective called her every day. It wasn't that she was romantically interested in the detective, but it was nice to know somebody cared not just about her mom's case but also what happened to Selena. He was like that overprotective uncle she never had. And it was cool that he was a homicide detective. She always thought she wanted to be a nurse or a doctor, but watching the police work her mother's case had her thinking maybe there were ways for her to help people other than going into medicine.

Zeek dragged the chair next to her and looked down at her homework. He grabbed the pen out of her hand and worked out the problem on her piece of paper. *Her* homework paper, that *she* had to turn in. Her teacher would know that wasn't her handwriting. Getting busted for cheating was the last thing she needed.

He sat up, said, "There, it's solved. Who's the man?" Obviously very proud of himself.

Selena rolled her eyes. "Oh, you're definitely the man." She was still irked by his comment about girls can't do math. Had he been kidding? He didn't seem to be joking. She'd let it go for now. They hadn't gotten into any fights for the last three days and she wasn't interested in starting a new one.

He continued to do her homework problems as if to show that he was really the mathematical genius he claimed to be. She had never questioned that Zeek was smart, but it was in no way cool that he was questioning her intelligence based on her gender. *Who does that?* And why was he continuing to do her homework? He wasn't even trying to teach her. He was simply showing off. It wasn't an attractive quality.

She supposed she should consider herself lucky that she had a smart boyfriend. Most of her friends dated such dummies. Mostly because they were good-looking. She was lucky to have a man that was both smart and good-looking. Her annoyance with him simmered down.

After watching him do her homework for ten minutes she said, "Okay, we need to leave for the police station." At first, she'd thought it was sweet how he'd insisted on taking her to the station for the lineup, but upon further thought she knew it was at least partially due to his jealousy. He didn't want her spending any alone time with the detective.

Selena and Zeek walked hand-in-hand into the police station. They were greeted by both Detective Renier and Detective Gates. Detective Gates introduced himself to Zeek, but Zeek mumbled and coldly shrugged it off, not even shaking the detective's hand. Selena watched as Gates's normal friendly demeanor toward her disappeared.

Detective Renier said, "Thank you for coming down, Selena. Are you ready?"

"I'm ready."

Detective Gates turned to Zeek. "I'm sorry to say, you can't come with us. You'll have to wait out here."

Selena suspected that Detective Gates wasn't sorry at all. She pried her hand away from Zeek's and before she could head off with the detectives, he kissed her on the lips, obviously marking his territory.

Selena let it slide as she and the detectives walked down the hallway until they reached a navy blue door. Detective Renier swiped a badge in front of a small black rectangle and held open the door for her. With rattling nerves, she crept in. She turned to the detectives. "He can't see me, right?"

"None of them will be able to see you. It's a one-way glass. Just take your time, Selena."

Selena continued in and stopped in front of the glass.

Detective Gates explained how the setup worked. She nodded in acknowledgment of what was about to happen. There was supposedly no reason to be afraid, but she was. Afraid of what she didn't know. He couldn't see her, but maybe she was afraid of what her reaction would be to seeing him. The man who killed her mother. She took a few cleansing breaths.

Detective Gates put his hand on her shoulder. "It'll be okay. They're gonna let them in now. Take your time."

She nodded.

She watched as six men entered one by one and turned to face her. Her heart sped up. *They can't see you, Selena.* She didn't need to take her time. Fox was man number two. She'd recognize his beady eyes anywhere. He was disgusting and sad looking. She hoped they locked him up and threw away the key. Or did to him what he had done to her mother. She turned to Detective Gates. "It's number two. Fox is number two."

Detective Renier asked, "Are you one hundred percent sure?"

"Positive. I've seen him multiple times. It's absolutely him. No question."

Detective Renier scribbled some notes in a folder and then handed it to Detective Gates. "Well done, Selena," Renier said.

"That's it?"

Detective Gates smiled. "Yep. Let's get you out of here."

The imaginary boulder on her back rolled off as she exited the room. As Detective Gates walked her back down the hall, Selena asked, "He'll go to jail forever, right?"

She waited for an answer longer than she'd have liked.

"We're pretty confident he's going to jail, but for how long, we're not sure. We'll try our best to get him locked away for a long time."

"Will I have to testify in court?"

"Yes, you will if it goes to trial."

Selena didn't like the sound of that, not one bit. It was bad enough seeing him through one-way glass. She'd be perfectly happy if she never saw his disgusting face ever again. But if she had to testify to make sure he got locked up, she'd do it. She'd be brave. She had to.

They shook hands and said their goodbyes.

Selena skittered over to Zeek, who was chewing on his fingernails. In an agitated tone he said, "You ready to go?"

"All done here." She smiled.

"Good." He sped out of the station.

She practically had to run after him to catch up. She hollered, "Wait up."

He got to the car and climbed in without a word. She slid into the passenger seat. "What's wrong with you?"

"I saw how he looked at you."

How he looked at me? Oh geez, not this again. She smiled sweetly. "Zeek, you know you're the only one for me. Don't be silly."

In a flash he had his hand on her neck and pushed her against the side of the car door. Through gritted teeth. He said, "Are you calling me a liar? I saw it with my eyes. Don't you ever call me a liar."

A mix of adrenaline, fear, and shock overtook her body. She clawed at his hand and gurgled, "Stop!"

He released her and faced straight ahead.

Selena put her hand to her neck where he had just had his. *This isn't happening. It can't be.*

Zeek bowed his head on the steering wheel, his chest heaving. He sat up and turned to her with tears flowing down his cheeks. "I'm so sorry. Oh my god. I don't know what came over me. I'm so sorry. Please say you'll forgive me. I don't know what I'd do without you. Babe?"

Selena stared at him with new eyes. "I forgive you. Please don't do it again. I love you." She knew better than to upset him further. If her mother was still alive, she'd thank her for that lesson.

"I love you too." He kissed her sweetly and refocused on the car. He turned the key and headed out of the police station parking lot.

They drove home in silence.

She tried to process what had just happened. How could he turn so cold so fast? He knew her mother had been strangled to death and he put his hands on her neck? She began adding up the events over the last week. Dread flooded her mind and her body. How had she been so stupid?

12

"Who can tell me the trigonometric function of theta equals pi over three?" The teacher paused. "Selena, how about you?"

Shit. "Sorry, what?"

Giggles and whispers from her classmates made it obvious she hadn't been paying attention. Apparently, it was funny to them that she was distracted by her mother's death and her angry boyfriend. The teacher looked at Alida sitting to Selena's right. "Alida, maybe you can help Selena? Can you tell us the trigonometric function of theta equals pi over three?"

Selena looked over at Alida with a pleading look. Alida said, "Sure ..."

That was something Selena had been pondering for days: Could Alida help her?

The day after her mother's death, Alida had said that she would ask her parents if Selena could stay with her family. Of course, Selena had adamantly refused, saying she had her wonderful boyfriend to live with. Alida hadn't brought it up again.

Selena assumed that Alida was too optimistic and that her

parents weren't willing to take in some orphaned teen for the rest of the school year. Alida's parents had always been polite and friendly when she visited their home. But deep down they probably thought Selena wasn't good enough to hang out with their only daughter.

She was trying to wrap her mind around the fact that Zeek wasn't Mr. Perfect after all. Mr. Not-Perfect was more appropriate. Alida had questioned how great he was from the very beginning, from that very first encounter at the coffee shop. How had Alida seen it, but Selena hadn't? Had she been wrong about Zeek? She was wrong, wasn't she? He was a bad guy, an abuser. If that was true, then why did she still want to be with him?

Since the incident in the police station parking lot the day before, he'd been attentive, sweet, and thoughtful. He'd even bought her flowers. Maybe she was overreacting? She still loved him even if he had a temper. His smile. His kiss. His arms around her. They were the best things she'd ever experienced in her whole life. She'd never felt more loved or wanted. After all, it was his jealousy that drove him to such anger.

Zeek was probably just stressed about finals. Selena hoped things would be better after the semester was over. It would be their first Christmas together and he'd told her he wanted her to come to his family's Christmas celebration so that she could meet them all. She was excited to meet his parents and brother and sister. From the sounds of things, he had a very normal family with a nice house in a nice neighborhood with Christmas trees and Christmas presents and relatives who ate a turkey feast together.

Relieved at the sound of the school bell, Alida and Selena walked side-by-side out of the classroom and toward the cafeteria. "Are you okay?" Alida asked.

"Yeah, it's just been it's been a long week, you know, with everything going on."

"I'm sorry. If there's anything you need or if you ever want to talk, you know I'm always here. You can tell me anything. I can be a good listener, I swear. Girl Scout's honor." Alida held up three fingers.

"Thanks."

They stepped into the crowded cafeteria and the smell of tater tots made Selena's stomach grumble. *Tater tots. Yes please.*

"How's Prince Charming?"

She smiled. "He's good." *Prince Charming?* Selena doubted Prince Charming ever choked out Cinderella. Ugh. She knew fairytales weren't real, so why was she hoping that Zeek and hers was?

They both stood in the long line.

"How's domestic bliss?"

Domestic bliss? It was bliss most of the time, wasn't it? Or was it just a ticking time bomb? Maybe she should talk to Alida about it. It would be nice to talk to someone about what was going on. She was probably overreacting, but it'd be nice to have a sounding board. "It's okay, he's just been really stressed. So he's kind of been short with me." Selena peaked at Alida's expression.

Her bubbly best friend turned very serious. "He hasn't hit you, has he? Or been violent?"

She swallowed.

Alida pressed. "Selena?"

She shook her head. "No, of course not. He's stressed out and we've had a few arguments. That's all. Finals are next week, so I'm sure things will get better after that."

"You'd tell me if he was hitting you, right?"

"Of course." More like she probably wouldn't. How embarrassing would that be? Selena had orchestrated her whole life to ensure she'd become the opposite of her mother. Now she had her first real boyfriend and he was acting like all of her mother's boyfriends. But he wasn't like them. He wasn't. It was only when he was mad. Most the time he was sweet and loving and complimented her constantly. Maybe the good outweighed the bad?

Is that what her mother had told herself too?

"Are you sure? You know, I spoke with my parents. You can stay with us. You don't have to live with him. Please, just stay with us. It'll be fun, I promise!" She batted her lashes at Selena.

Should I? How would Zeek react? Would he break up with me? Selena forced a smile. "Really, I'm okay. I like living with Zeek. It's okay, I swear."

Alida sighed and then shifted her tone. "I can't wait for some tater tots. How about you?"

"Totally. My mouth is watering."

Her thoughts returned to Zeek. It wasn't like he'd tried to kill her. He was just angry and pushed her. She loved him. He loved her. It was so confusing. Maybe they needed to have a heart-to-heart after finals. Or maybe see a counselor. That was normal, right? Was it normal after dating for only six weeks?

Selena stood at the front of her school waiting for Zeek to pick her up. She'd thought it over and convinced herself that she'd overreacted. Zeek wasn't like Debbie's boyfriends. She spotted his dark gray Honda approaching and grinned. She would make this work. This wasn't like her mother and her abuser boyfriends. She and Zeek were different. This was love. She opened the door and slid in. She leaned over to give him a peck on the lips. He blocked her mouth with his hand and sat back. Selena's mouth gaped open. "What's wrong?"

"What's wrong?"

"Yeah, what's wrong?"

"Who's that guy you were standing with?"

Selena cocked her head and then turned to look out the window. A couple of guys were standing close to where she had been. "Those guys there? I wasn't talking to them."

The storm returned to his normally calm blue eyes. "Don't lie to me."

"I'm not lying to you. I don't even know them. I think they're in a grade or two below me. I wasn't talking to them, I swear." She hoped he believed her. The storm remained. Her pulse quickened. *Please, don't. Please.*

"If you don't know them, how do you know they're a grade below you?"

"I said I think they are. I don't even know their names."

"Are you fucking them?"

She shook her head in disbelief. "No, God, no, Zeek. That's ..." She now knew to not use the word *silly* or *crazy* or anything that would indicate she was calling him a name. She knew what happened when she did.

Zeek glared at her. "You're a fucking whore. You want them, go have them. Get the fuck out of my car!"

Selena panicked. "Zeek, I swear to God, I wasn't talking to them."

He shouted, "Get out!"

She opened the door. With one leg outside he pushed her back and she stumbled out of the car, the contents of her bag spilling on the pavement.

By the time she stood up and collected her things, he had driven out of the school parking lot. She looked up at the boys Zeek had accused her of fraternizing with. They were staring at her. One of them ran up to her. "Are you okay? Who was that?"

Her cheeks burned. "Oh, it was just my brother. It's fine, we're just having a family spat. Brothers are such jerks. I'm fine, really. Thank you for asking." Selena tried to fight the tears that were threatening to be unleashed. She collected her backpack and keys that had fallen out and started walking toward the bus stop. She held her head high, as if nothing horribly embarrassing or shameful had just happened.

In that moment, she knew she wasn't overreacting. The man she loved had hurt her. What could she do to get away from him? Maybe she could find her dad? Sure, he was probably shooting up somewhere, but maybe being with him was better than being abused by her boyfriend. She squeezed her eyes shut. It was her worst fear coming to fruition. She had become just like her.

13

Selena wrinkled her nose and shifted her gaze out the bus window. She hated taking the public bus. The smell of dried vomit and body odor made her want to gag. Not that she had any other choice. Zeek couldn't know where she was going and what she was doing. Sure, when she finally made it home the night before, Zeek had apologized, begged for forgiveness, and said he'd turned his car around nearly instantly but couldn't find her. She wasn't sure if that was true, but his new pattern of flipping out on her and then apologizing, crying and begging for her forgiveness, had gotten old fast. She would not stay with an abuser. She'd worked too hard to simply end up like her mother. It broke her heart to think she wouldn't have Zeek in her life anymore, but she wouldn't become one of those women. A statistic. She shut her eyes and reopened them. It was too late, she had become one of those women, but she wouldn't let it continue. She wouldn't let it ruin her life.

Where would she go? Should she just get over herself and tell Alida that she would move in with her and her family? She could do that, or she could find her father. She wanted to find her father, he was the only family she had left. Maybe he had an apartment somewhere and she could stay with him until she went off to college. The only challenge: finding him.

The bus halted and the doors chugged open. She climbed out of her seat and descended the steps onto the sidewalk. Head high, she strutted toward the entrance of the police station and walked through the automatic doors. She approached the reception window.

"How can I help you?"

"I'm here to see Detective Gates."

"Name."

Selena was starting to see that not all police officers were friendly, certainly not this guy. He was probably disgruntled that he had to work the front desk.

"Selena Bailey."

Obviously bothered by her presence, he asked, "What is this about?"

She spat. "My mother's homicide."

The officer's face softened. "I'll call him. You can take a seat over there along the wall."

She wondered how long she'd be able to play the *my mother's been murdered* card. It would probably shut everyone up. No one knew what to say to her after that, and she didn't know what to say back, so it worked out fine.

She wandered over to the dark wooden chairs and sat to wait for the detective. Would he be able to help her find her dad? She hoped so. He'd been helpful up until this point. She glanced up at the sound of her name from a familiar voice. Detective Gates stood there in his usual dark slacks with a dark polo shirt showing off his muscles. He definitely worked out. She now saw why Zeek had been jealous. Detective Gates was pretty good-looking for an old guy. She stood up. "Hi, Detective Gates."

"I wasn't expecting you, but I was just about to call you. Why don't you come back to my desk."

She nodded and followed him.

She sat in the chair next to his desk as he reviewed some papers. "What were you going to call me about?"

"Well, let me see here. Yes, okay, so it's about your mother. The medical examiner is ready to release her body. We haven't been able to locate any of your mother's relatives. Although we do believe that you have relatives out there. We just haven't been able to find them yet. The last known addresses and phone numbers didn't work or were out of date. We can keep looking, or, since you're the only identifiable next of kin, the decision falls on you."

She shook her head. "Decision? I don't understand what you're asking me."

"I'm sorry. Typically what happens is the family at this point would request the body be transferred to a mortuary for funeral preparations."

Funeral preparations. It hadn't crossed her mind. *Who would even come?* "Sounds expensive. I don't really have money for that. What happens if you don't have money for that?" It appeared she could sink lower. Who didn't have enough money to bury their own mother? She had some savings, but this might clean her out. Right now, she needed all the funds she could get her hands on.

"Funerals can be costly. We're talking anywhere from five to ten grand for a funeral. What happens when the family doesn't intend to claim the body or can't afford to, is the county cremates the remains and puts them in a cardboard box and sends them to storage. If you claim the remains, there is a fee usually just under two hundred dollars. You can also choose to get some sort of container other than a cardboard box, for a price. Some people like to get the ashes and spread them in the ocean or in their loved one's favorite place."

Like mixed in her favorite cocktail? Now that was awful. Selena shook herself. Did her mom have a favorite place? She didn't think so, but she also didn't think she wanted to leave her mom in a cardboard box in a police storage unit. She would have to take the money out of savings. She didn't have much left, but she couldn't just leave her mom in a storage room among the unloved and unclaimed. "I can't afford a funeral and all that other stuff, but I would like her ashes and maybe something nicer than a cardboard box. Do you know how much that usually costs?"

"It varies. I'll get you the information for the company that takes care of the arrangements."

"Okay." More expenses. She'd have to increase her hours at the restaurant, which she should do anyway. She needed money now more than ever. She couldn't depend on Zeek. Not for a place to live, not for anything.

Detective Gates looked at her with an odd look in his eyes. Pity? Concern? He said, "I'll keep you updated on the case against Fox. We're hoping it doesn't go to trial, but you never know. The DA will try to get him to take a plea. Right now he's not cooperating, so it's too soon to tell. But if you have any questions, you can call me anytime."

She nodded and watched him intently as she gathered the courage to ask him if he'd help her. It was the only reason she'd come down to the station during her lunch period.

"You came down here for a reason. Was it to ask about your mother's case or was there something else?" the detective asked.

She bit her lower lip. "Yeah, I was hoping you could help me find my dad. He's most likely somewhere in the Bay Area."

Detective Gates shifted in his chair as if he was contemplating the request. Did he not want to help her?

"When you came in here the first time to give a statement, you didn't seem like you wanted to have anything to do with your father. Has something changed?"

She fiddled with the ring on her finger. "I don't know that something's changed. I just wonder if maybe it's better that I live with him instead of Zeek, because, you know, I just applied for schools and I'll have to submit my FAFSAs and will need his information. That sort of stuff. And ... I only have one parent now and I figure maybe having him is better than having no one." She averted her gaze to the floor as the tears welled. She felt silly. Every time she sat in the chair next to the detective she broke down. It was as if in front of everyone else she'd held the steely exterior. Something about Detective Gates made her tell the truth, which ultimately made her fall apart. Maybe she sensed that he was a protective force, someone who didn't harm people. He was someone who helped people. She accepted his latest offering of a tissue. She dried her eyes and looked up at him. "Sorry."

"No need to apologize. I'll help you find your dad. Here's a piece of paper, write down everything you remember about him and everything you know about him. It'll be okay."

She didn't believe he had the power to know that. She wasn't sure that everything would be okay. How was he so sure? He didn't know her or her life. Maybe she should stay with Alida until they found her dad. She'd think about it.

She took the pen and wrote down everything she could remember about her father. His full name and where he was the last time she saw him. She could feel the detective watching her.

She finished writing and slid the paper across the desk. "Will you be able to find him?"

He studied the paper for a moment. "If he's around, we'll find him. What made you decide to come down here during the day, shouldn't you be in school?"

She said, "I thought maybe it would be easier if I came down here by myself, that's all. It's my lunch period right now."

He spoke in a soothing tone. "Selena, is there anything else you want to ask me or anything else I can do for you today?"

Selena looked down at the yellow gold band on his ring finger. She wondered how he treated his wife. Was he always this calm with her or was he a Zeek, acting like he was loving, strong, and careful, but at the drop of a pin could turn into a monster?

"No, that's it. Thank you. When should I come back to find out if you found my dad?"

"It might take a little while to locate him, but how about you come back on Monday during your lunch?" Two more days. She'd be okay for two more days. She would just make sure she didn't do anything to upset Zeek.

"Well, thank you again, Detective Gates. I really appreciate it." She stood up from the chair and was about to head out when he stopped her. "Can I give you a ride back to school?"

She checked the time on her phone. There was no chance Zeek would be around, he had class until two. "Yeah, thanks."

On the drive back to school, Detective Gates asked her about her classes and her plans for college. He told her he was impressed by her and that he thought she had a bright future. She hoped he was right, and she hoped he could find her father because if Detective Gates couldn't, Selena didn't know what she'd do.

14

Sunday morning Selena smiled as she felt Zeek squeeze her tight. Her eyes widened and smile faded as her mind returned to reality. Why couldn't he just get his anger under control? He was so wonderful when he wasn't angry. She knew there wasn't anything she could do, though. It was time to be brave.

She knew fate might leave her alone in this increasingly dark world, but she also knew she couldn't stay in this relationship. The zillion-dollar question was how would she leave without him realizing her intentions?

Ironically, her mother's favorite TV station had been Lifetime. Selena had seen her fair share of made-for-TV movies featuring a battered wife who tried to leave and was promptly murdered by her used-to-be-so-loving husband. The public service announcement at the end usually featured a hotline number to call and warnings about domestic violence. Between her real-life experience and the trillion movies she watched since birth, how had she ended up lying next to a man like that?

One thing that had always stuck in the back of her mind was that when an abuser thinks you're leaving, that's when they strike hardest. Not that she really thought that Zeek was capable of murder, but better safe than sorry. She'd miss him. She'd miss him *a lot*.

She turned over, facing him, and planted a kiss on his lips. "I wish we could lie here all day."

He ran his fingers through her hair and said, "Why can't we?"

"For one, I have to go to work, and two, we have to study for finals. Ugh, three, I need to finish my senior project. Maybe after finals we can have a day of laying about all day." It was a promise she knew she'd never fulfill.

He leaned back. "You have to work today? I thought you were off."

"Yeah, I asked my boss to increase my hours if they could. I need the money."

"I thought we talked about this already. You don't need to work extra hours. I can take care of you."

A chill ran through her. She needed to defuse the bomb that was about to go off. When she'd increased her hours, she'd anticipated he might be upset and so she hadn't told him. She hadn't realized he'd memorized her schedule. "I know you can, it's just that I was talking to the detective—" She paused. *Fuck.* The detective was another trigger and she hadn't told him that she had gone down to the police station. "He said that I have to claim my mother's body and I opted to have her cremated. It costs a lot of money. I didn't want you to have to pay for my mother's remains, you know."

She watched and waited. Maybe he was too tired to fight. Or maybe he was contemplating his attack.

He squinted his eyes at her and shut them and then opened them again. "When did you talk to the detective?"

Bad sign. "On Friday. The medical examiner was ready to

release my mom's body and he needed to know what to do with it."

"Why didn't you tell me this before? What else are you hiding?"

"I'm not hiding anything. I just tried to put it out of my mind. It's upsetting to think about having to claim my mother's dead body. I didn't want to think about it, let alone talk about it."

He wasn't simmering down. He was firing up. He sat upright in the bed. "I don't like you keeping things from me. I don't keep things from you. For us to be in a relationship, we have to have trust and I'm starting to really not trust you."

Shit. She sat up, covering herself with the light gray sheets. "You can trust me. I'm not hiding anything, I swear. Full disclosure, the detective said he would continue to keep in contact while they were putting together the case against Fox. I may have to testify in court."

His shoulders seemed to relax. Relief filled her. She smiled and put her arms around his neck. "I love you so much, Zeek."

He wrapped his arms around her. "I love you too, babe."

After a rumble and tumble in the sheets, she watched as Zeek moseyed into the bathroom. At the sound of the shower spray, she jumped out of bed and checked the time on her phone. She had twenty minutes to get ready for work, which meant no time for a shower. She slipped on her work clothes as Zeek re-entered the bedroom. "Where are you going?"

"To work."

"I told you you didn't need to work extra hours."

Selena froze. *It was back. The rage.*

"But I have a shift, I can't just not show up. I'll tell them to reduce my hours. It's fine, but I have to go now. I don't want to get fired."

He stalked toward her. "Who cares if they fire you? I can take care of you. Do you not believe that I can take care of you?"

"No, I believe you. I actually think you can. I don't want you to have to do everything. I love you and want to be your partner, not just someone you take care of."

"I want you to quit your job. Just school. I'll take care of you. I'm the man and I will take care of you."

Holy Batman, he is a misogynist. Her stomach curdled. She shoved her feelings down and smiled sweetly. "I know you can, and I appreciate that. How about this, I'll go in today and give my notice."

He tipped his chin and looked at her with the devil in his eyes. "No, that doesn't work for me. You said you'd like to spend all day in bed, so that's what you'll do. I want to give you everything you've ever wanted. How does that sound?"

Really fucking bad. "I love that idea, Zeek, it would be a dream come true. Let me just go in today and finish my shift. I'd hate to leave them short-staffed with no notice. After that I'll quit, and then next Sunday we can spend all day in bed." She was finding it increasingly more difficult to play the loving girlfriend.

"I said no. You're not going anywhere even if I have to tie you to that bed."

Was that a threat? How had she been so stupid as to get herself into this situation? Her phone buzzed, but before she could see who was calling, Zeek grabbed it out of her hand. He sneered. "Oh, it looks like your precious detective is calling you. Shall I answer it for you, or would you prefer to answer it yourself?"

She shook her head. "I'm sure it's nothing. Either he'll leave a message or I can call him later."

He chucked the phone to the ground. She had wanted a clean, calculated plan to exit his life, but now she knew she was better off making a run for it. It was decided, as soon as she got to work, she'd call Alida and tell her that she would stay with Alida's family.

He wasn't backing down. "What's the matter? No sweet nothings for the detective?" Zeek's eyes went ice cold. "Why don't you make yourself comfortable and lay down, babe."

Selena stiffened.

"Didn't you hear me?" He shoved her onto the bed with the force of a comet. She cried out in pain and clasped her chest with her hands.

He said, "Take off your clothes."

She slipped off her skirt and unbuttoned her blouse and tossed them on the floor.

"The rest."

With trembling hands, she unclasped her bra and slid off her underwear. She vowed not to cry.

"Now don't go anywhere."

He exited the room. Her mind raced and fear swelled inside of her. She eyed her phone on the floor and contemplated picking it up and calling for help. Help from what? He hadn't hit her. Not yet.

He came back in the room with a devilish grin and hatred in his eyes. "Babe, we're about to have some fun."

She studied the rope in his hand and her body became paralyzed. He was going to do it. He was going to tie her up. What was the right move? It was like when you spotted a bear. Are you supposed to act big or play dead? She said, "Zeek, this really isn't necessary. I'll stay home. It's fine."

"No, no. I think this will be fun. Trust me."

A sickening realization shot through her. *He enjoyed making her squirm.*

Selena awoke the next morning, wrists still tied to the bed post. The previous day's events flashed through her memory. She'd begged and pleaded for him to untie her, but he'd laughed it off, said they were having fun. She didn't want to anger him, so she'd finally submitted. She had been relieved when Zeek had left her after the second time he'd had his way with her. She wasn't sure if he'd slept on the futon in the living room or if he'd actually left the apartment. She didn't know what time it was, all she could tell from the sunlight filtering in through the blinds was that it was daytime. She didn't hear any other noises in the apartment. How long would he leave her tied up? How would she go to school or meet the detective to see if he had found her father? Dread filled her belly. What if he never intended to let her go?

15

Selena studied the room. He hadn't covered her mouth. She could scream for help, but what he if he was right outside? Her wrists and ankles burned from the rope and her chest ached from where he shoved her. She'd always been sure life would get better and that she wasn't destined to repeat the mistakes of her mother. Now she wasn't sure about anything. Maybe a happy life wasn't in the cards, not for her. Maybe this was her fate.

She heard the jingle of the front door lock and her body tensed. Moments later, Zeek entered the bedroom with a sweet smile on his face and a white bag. "You're up." He slithered over to the bed, bent over, and kissed her on the lips. "Good morning, babe. I just went out for breakfast. I brought you something back. Let me get you untied. I would've done it earlier, but you were sleeping so soundly, I didn't want to disturb you."

Didn't want to disturb me? But you're perfectly fine with tying me up against my will? Right. She eked out a "Thanks."

Selena assumed Zeek had anger-management issues, but now she considered the possibility that he was fucking crazy. He was talking to her as if they were literally playing a game and that she was sleeping so soundly he didn't want to untie her restraints. Didn't he see the rope burns and dark bruising on her chest?

She flinched as he approached with a pocketknife, assuming he was going to cut her, but he didn't. Instead, he cut the rope and freed her.

"Can I take a shower?" she asked.

He laughed. "Of course."

She faked a weak grin and scampered to the bathroom and shut the door. Of all the nightmares she had growing up, none of them looked like this. What the hell was she going to do?

She showered quickly, not looking at her bruises, and slurped water from the tap. Then she exited the bathroom and put on some clothes that were lying on the floor. She searched the flooring for the pieces of her phone. Maybe it would still work. She peeked over at him. "Where's my phone?"

"I thought it would be kind of fun to go low-tech today, don't you?"

Low-tech? She didn't like the sound of that. It sounded a lot like he was keeping her phone from her. "Without my phone I don't even know what time it is. What time is it? I need to go to school."

"You probably missed first period, but if you hurry up, you'll make it to second. I can drop you off."

Just like that? One thing was for sure, he could drop her off, but there was no way she was going back with him. *Never, ever. Ever.* She said, "Okay, great. Thank you."

It baffled Selena that Zeek had two completely different personas. He was a loving boyfriend one moment and became a deranged freak at the drop of a hat. She needed to get away from both of them and fast.

She now knew, no question, she couldn't stay a moment longer with Zeek. As soon as she got her phone back or she saw Alida at school—whichever came first—she would talk to her about moving in with her family until they located her father. At lunch, she would meet with Detective Gates. Hopefully he'd found her father and she could stay with him. No, it wasn't too late for her. She wouldn't give up yet. She would escape from this person. This person she thought she'd loved.

"I planned on being close by anyways. I'll pick you up after school too. I'm a full-service boyfriend today!"

Her heart froze. He wasn't letting her out of his sight. She wondered if he somehow knew that she'd gone to the police station on Friday. Okay. She could still do this. At school, she'd borrow Alida's phone and call the detective to explain the situation.

"I can take the bus if you have other things to do."

He grabbed her by the waistline. "No, it's okay. I like being close to you."

As she suppressed the vomit in her throat, she said, "I like being close to you too."

On the drive to school, she munched on the maple donut he had brought her while she thought of all the ways she could pretend like everything was okay so as not to alert him that she was going make a run for it. They approached the exit to her high school, but instead of veering right he turned to her and smiled. "I have a surprise for you."

Why wasn't he taking her to school? Where was he taking her? "Oh, a surprise, I love surprises. But I have a test today." She didn't have a test, but she was far from interested in any more of his surprises.

"Oh, I'm sure you can make it up. It will be fine. I wanted to show you something really special. I realized the other day that you and I have never been to the lake. Do you like the lake?"

Had Zeek had some sort of psychotic break? "What lake do you mean?"

"Lake Tahoe of course! You've been there right? Isn't it beautiful?"

Of course? Of course, the lake that was four hours away? "Yes, it's stunning. A bit chilly this time of the year. Isn't it snowing?"

"Yes, I love the snow. It's so pristine. My family has a cabin with views of the lake. Best of all, it's really isolated with nobody around for miles. You and I can really spend some quality alone time."

Sweat was building on her brow. This was bad, very fucking bad. "Sounds romantic. I'm not sure today is a great day for it, though. I have finals and my senior project due this week. Maybe after school's out for winter break, we can visit and maybe spend a whole week there. That would be amazing. I've never stayed at a cabin on Lake Tahoe before. It's so sweet of you to want to bring me there." She hoped flattery would get her somewhere—more specifically, anywhere Zeek wouldn't be.

A glimmer of hope sparked inside of her. If she missed her appointment with the detective, maybe he would realize something was wrong and come looking for her? *Keep positive, Selena, it's not over yet.* Maybe she was overreacting? Or maybe he liked tying her up and needed a secluded location to have more of his twisted fun. What else was he planning? She shuddered at the vile images racing through her brain as Zeek continued to drive them away from her school.

16

Detective Ed Gates eyed the couple approaching him and his partner Thursday morning. The woman stood a good three inches taller than the man, who was a bit round with dark hair and eyes. Both looked a little rough around the edges. Perhaps former addicts. Ed wondered if addicts realized that a trained eye could spot them a mile away. "I'm Detective Gates and this is my partner Detective Renier."

Everyone shook hands.

"Thank you for agreeing to see me. As I mentioned on the phone, I'm Martina Monroe, I'm a security specialist and private investigator. This is my fiancé, Charlie Bailey."

Selena had her father's eyes, Ed realized. Selena had thought her dad was still an addict, but Ed wasn't so sure. The man was wearing clean clothes and was engaged to a woman associated with law enforcement and, by the way she held herself, maybe ex-military. He said, "I see. I've actually been looking for you, Charlie. Selena had asked that I try to locate you after her mother's death."

There was notable pain in Charlie's eyes. He frowned. "As soon as I heard Debbie had died, I started going out of my mind wondering what's happened to Selena. I had no idea until just a few days ago."

Martina explained. "We found out about Debbie's death through one of my contacts who was investigating a related matter. I told Charlie about the case and he asked what had happened to Selena, but we couldn't find anything to indicate where she may be staying. A friend found out that you were looking for Charlie, so we figured we'd reach out in person."

Ed thought, *She has a friend who has eyes on police records? Who is this woman?*

Charlie's face screamed desperation. "Do you know where she is or where she's staying?"

Selena had missed their appointment on Monday. Ed's gut had been telling him something was very wrong. He didn't like Selena's skittish behavior when she'd been down to the station the previous Friday or the fact that she had felt she needed to come alone, without the boyfriend. He didn't like that Zeek character from day one. He hoped the background on Zeek would come back and prove that his instinct was wrong, but Ed knew that wasn't likely and it scared the living hell out of him. Ed said, "I haven't seen her since Friday."

"But you know where she's staying? Where she's been?" Charlie asked.

Ed feared the worry on his face showed like a neon sign. "Not exactly. She was supposed to meet me on Monday for an update on your location, but she didn't show. She hasn't been answering my phone calls, either. I called her school and she hasn't been to school since last Friday. We conducted a welfare check at the apartment where she had been staying with her boyfriend. Nobody's home."

Martina stood with her hands on her hips. "Who is this boyfriend?"

"His name is Zeek Tate. He's twenty-two years old, or so he

says. I get the impression they haven't been together long, maybe two months. I'm running a background right now. I'm not gonna lie. I am concerned."

"Is it unusual for her not to take your calls?" Martina asked.

"It is. Since her mother's death, I've called her at least once a day to check in on her to make sure she's all right. Good kid, but the boyfriend ... I'm not so sure." He didn't want to be right about Zeek, because if he was, it meant major trouble for Selena. It didn't feel right that Selena hadn't shown up on Monday or hadn't been to school in three days. Last they spoke, Selena had been excited about college, had already submitted her applications, and was finishing up her senior project. It didn't make sense she would just disappear.

Lenny, an analyst from downstairs, approached their desks "Hey boss, I got the report you asked for. I think you'll want to take a look at it."

Ed didn't need to be a detective to know it was not good news. "Time is of the essence, can you give us the CliffsNotes version?"

Lenny nodded and focused on the paper. "Zeek Tate, twenty-two, originally from Ridgemont. Straight A student in high school, accepted into UC Berkeley but dropped out two years ago after his girlfriend went missing. She hasn't been found. There was some suspicion about him being involved, but rumors are that family money squashed any bad press. He doesn't have a job but takes a few classes at the local junior college. Financials would indicate he lives off an allowance from his parents."

Ed wanted to punch a wall. He *knew* there was something up with that guy. He should've kept a closer eye on Selena. If something happened to Selena, it would be his fault.

"Thanks, Lenny." He looked over at his partner. "We need to find Selena. Let's put out a BOLO on Zeek's car and find out if his family owns any property in and around the area. Lenny, buddy, can you get on it ASAP?"

"Sure thing, boss. I'll get to it now. I'll let you know as soon as I find something." Lenny rushed back down the hall.

Ed eyed Martina. She took a step closer and spoke quietly. "In my line of business, we have a way of getting information very quickly, but not necessarily in methods that are approved by the police department. If you share some information about this Zeek guy with me, I might be able to find Selena faster than you or your department could, but you can't ask any questions."

He stared straight into her amber eyes. "Do it." They had to find her, by *any means necessary.*

17

___

Selena tried to wipe the tears from her cheeks onto the pillow. How long would he keep her tied up? She'd never been afraid to die before. She always had the idea that when her time came, it was her time, and she would be okay with that. That type of thinking allowed her to survive the nights when her mother's latest boyfriend would scare her through the walls or up close and personal. She wasn't sure if she believed in God, but she had always believed there was a plan for her life and those around her. But, if there was a God, why would he allow people like Zeek to prey on women, tie them up like they were their property instead of human beings, capable and strong? He was going to kill her. She knew it in her bones.

She laughed at herself for being so naive. She had said she'd never, ever be like her mother. Here she was a full eighteen years ahead of Debbie. At least her mother lived to thirty-five. She wished her mother was with her now.

She looked blindly around the bedroom of Zeek's parents' cabin. Despite being tied to the bed, she could see out the window. It was snowing. She had never seen a white Christmas and depending on when Zeek planned to end her life, she may never get to. Deep down, she knew he'd never let her go. The first day she'd pleaded and begged him to untie her. She swore she wouldn't run away. She tried to remain sweet and keep on his good side to convince him that she still loved him, but realized before the day was even up that it was all in vain. He was a monster, and monsters didn't let their prey go.

She had endured the last three days mostly by staring out the window pretending she was outside. The fluttering snowflakes and sparkling lake were magical—a stark contrast to inside, where everything was dark and depraved.

A little yellow bird landed on a branch, staring at her like it was trying to communicate a message. Its eyes transfixed on her. She wanted to be that bird. She did want to be free. She couldn't give up. She had to fight. But how?

The creak of footsteps approaching the bedroom door drew her gaze to the left. He was coming back. With that creepy smile, the same one she used to find so dazzling, he said, "Good morning babe. I made us some coffee. Unfortunately, no Frappuccinos out here."

She forced her lips to curl up words. "Thank you, good morning to you too. It looks beautiful outside. Maybe later we can go for a walk."

Zeek set the coffee on the nightstand and sat on the edge of the bed. He bent down and kissed her. She kissed him back with as much enthusiasm as she could muster. What once made her quiver with desire now made her stomach revolt.

He sat back. "You seem tense. Are you not enjoying our role-playing? You know, all couples role-play, that's how they keep the passion alive. I wanna see you smile. Smile for me."

She smiled a toothy grin. She was convinced he knew it was forced, adding to his pleasure. "I'm having fun, but I'm thinking maybe, it would be even more fun if we could dance together or make breakfast together or something. You know, other than just laying in this old bed." She tried to add a chipper tone to her voice. "Also, I'm really starting to stink. Wouldn't you enjoy a more fresh-scented Selena?"

He hunched over her and sniffed her neck and then continued sniffing down her naked body until he reached her center. He looked up and said, "You are a bit ripe."

She wondered how he could possibly be turned on by this. She hadn't showered in three days and was using a mixing bowl as a toilet.

He sat up. "Let me think about this. I would hate for you to stop playing with me."

She shook her head. "I'm not going anywhere sweetheart. I love you. I'd never leave you. You're the love of my life. I can't wait for the day we can get married and have a family."

"Let me think." He looked her up and down and then briskly exited the room.

She wondered what he had in mind. Surely it wasn't something like, *just kidding, game's over, you're free now.* Whatever he came back with would be terrible, but she wasn't sure it could be worse than being tied to the fucking bed.

She looked around the room for possible weapons. There was a lamp on each nightstand. A chair. Not much else.

When they had first arrived, he gave her a tour of the house. It had three bedrooms, a living room, a den with a flat-screen TV and comfy sofas, and a decent-sized kitchen. When she saw it, all her fears had slipped away. She thought maybe he really was taking her away for a romantic getaway to make up for restraining her the night before. Even with being tied to their bed back at the apartment, she never would've imagined this.

The kitchen seemed well-stocked. If she could get to the kitchen she could find a weapon. He was bigger and he was clever, but she'd survived too much for her life to end this way.

He returned seemingly empty-handed. "Just so we're clear, I'm in charge. It's the rules of the game, okay?"

She nodded quickly. "Of course, you're in charge."

He approached the bed and pulled a black gun from the waistband of his pants and aimed it at her.

She squeezed her eyes shut. *Oh God, he's gonna kill me right now and there's nothing I can do about it.*

He moved closer and put the muzzle of the gun on the side of her head and proceeded to trace it down her cheek, her neck, her collarbone, and down the side of her body.

She thought she was going to throw up. He leaned over and kissed her belly button. Her body twitched, rejecting his touch.

He glared up at her. "Just another prop for our game to make sure everyone abides by the rules. I hope you follow the rules, I really do. I'm having way too much fun to end things now."

He put the gun back in his waistband and began untying the restraints. She couldn't quite reach the lamp. It was too big and bulky to use as a weapon anyways. Maybe when she was untied, she could run. A moving target was more difficult to shoot. But she was also naked, and it was snowing outside. If he didn't kill her, the elements would. She couldn't run. She'd have to fight him.

Removing the last of her ankle restraints. He said, "Let's get you cleaned up."

She was so stunned she didn't respond.

He demanded. "C'mon. Up now."

She flung her legs over the bed and used the mattress to steady herself. She hadn't walked in three days and her legs were weak. She zombie walked into the small adjoining bathroom and turned on the shower. She stepped in and went to pull the curtain shut when he said, "No, no, I want to watch you."

She forced a smile and tugged the curtain back. She lathered as he stared, gun in hand. She'd never been more terrified in her entire life, and she realized now that was really saying something.

She had succeeded in convincing him to untie her. It was a small win. Next, she had to get him to give her access to the kitchen. She'd get a hold of a knife or something sharp. She could then use the element of surprise. First, knee him in the balls and then stab him in the eye. Then grab his keys and take the car. Drive away. No stopping. Drive all the way back to the police station in Grapton Hill.

She turned off the water, grabbed the towel on the hook, and wrapped it around herself before stepping onto the bright green bathmat. "Can I put my clothes back on? It's cold in here."

"Sure. But I have something else for you to wear too." From his pocket, he pulled a spool of fishing line. *Not good news.*

He knelt down, tucked the gun into the back of his jeans, and looped the fishing line around her ankle. Was this her opportunity to smash his face with her foot? Too risky. She had no follow-up weapon.

He tied it then walked back over to the bed and tied it to the bed frame. He smiled up at her. "Now you can walk around the house. We can dance and pretend like we're married, spending our first Christmas together as husband and wife. You'd be making me breakfast as we talked about how many children to have. At least one boy and one girl. I can picture it now, my wife, in her rightful place: at home taking care of the kids and all my needs."

She was definitely ready to kill this asshole.

"That sounds amazing. I look forward to that. One day after we're done with school and—" Her agreeing to this fantasy life was stopped short by his howling laughter.

He said, "Babe, there's no need for you to go to college. I'll make the money, I'll take care of all of us."

"Oh wow, I hadn't realized that's what our marriage would be like. It sounds so ... nice." *Nice, like, if you think it would be nice to spend your life with a psychotic husband and a few of his demented offspring.* This guy, this product of the patriarchy, would *not* be the end of her. She was ready to fight. Fight to the death, if necessary. She said, "I'm starved. Are there groceries so I can cook us some breakfast? Maybe eggs and toast?" She really only knew how to cook eggs, fingers crossed that was what he had.

"Sure, let's get you dressed. I have eggs, toast, bacon, and I even got you an apron."

An apron, just what I've always wanted. Not. She dressed quickly to ensure he didn't change his mind about letting her roam around. She forced a grin, happy to at least be clean and covered. "All set. Let's make breakfast."

She scooted out of the bedroom, down the hall, and then stepped into the L-shaped kitchen with an island in the center. She didn't see a knife block on the counter. *They must be in the drawer.* Her nerves rattled as she replayed the plan in her head. Would she be able to pull it off? Only one way to find out.

She went to the refrigerator and pulled out a carton of eggs, a package of bacon, and the bread, butter, and milk. She set them on the counter and started humming "Bad Romance" by Lady Gaga to calm her nerves.

She opened the drawer to look for utensils. There weren't any knives, but there was a plethora of spoons and forks. She'd have to make do. A fork to the eye was probably as bad as a knife, right? She grabbed the fork and started whisking the eggs in a bowl similar to the one she had been using as a toilet. She felt bile rising in her throat.

Zeek approached her from behind, putting his hands on her waist, and started kissing her neck. If she weren't being held hostage, it would've been kind of romantic, but since she was being held hostage - not so much. A homicidal rage swirled inside her. It was now or never. She turned around and smiled, fork in hand. She kissed him and pushed him back up against the refrigerator to give herself more leverage to hit him as hard as she could.

He smiled sweetly at her as if he wasn't a psychopath and said, "I love you."

She smirked. "I love you too, *babe*." And kneed him in the testicles as hard as she could. As he bent over in pain, grabbing his crotch, she rammed the fork toward his eye and missed. *Shit.* She tried again and again, but he batted her away. He went for his gun as she threw her clenched fists at him. The gun slid out of his pants and hit the tile floor with a crack. She scrambled after it. He tackled her and flipped her over. She lay on her back as he straddled her, gun pressed against her forehead. "You bitch!"

She squeezed her eyes shut and silently begged him not to kill her.

18

DETECTIVE ED GATES

E d slammed on the horn. Downtown Lake Tahoe was jam-packed with tourist who didn't know how to drive worth a damn. They were too preoccupied with sipping their hot cocoa to pay attention to the road. No mind to the fact that a young girl could be in danger. Martina said, "Hey, getting into an accident won't get us there any faster. Are you sure you don't want me to drive?"

"I'm fine. You just hold your horses, buddy."

Martina appeared to be worried about her future stepdaughter, but she also didn't know the whole story. If she did, she'd be terrified. He hadn't wanted to alert Selena's father, Charlie, or Martina about the vibe he'd gotten off Zeek almost immediately. He knew enough predators in his day to suspect that Zeek was part of that fucked-up club. It was one of the reasons he'd insisted on keeping in contact with Selena. He didn't trust that guy from day one.

Ed also hadn't told Martina and Charlie that Selena had confessed that it was better for her to talk to him alone *without Zeek around*. He should've done more drive-bys. He should've checked up on her more. If this ended badly, it was on him.

He wasn't thrilled to be traveling to a potential crime scene with a civilian, but considering Martina's team had found the information on Zeek and his family's property holdings quicker than the department had, he couldn't exactly tell her no. Plus, if they did find Selena, he was pretty sure she'd be damn happy to see her dad.

Martina said, "We should come up with a plan for an organized approach. I already have a few guys coming in from the Bay Area as backup."

Guys for backup? This woman was trying to take over his investigation. She had balls, that was for sure. Normally he'd be pissing all over his territory, but he wanted to find Selena alive. Preferably unharmed. He'd let Martina's power trip slide for now. "Agreed. The local sheriff and PD have been notified that there may be a need for backup."

Martina said, "The intelligence I received says the house is located down a private road, about a half mile from the main highway. I don't want to notify him of our presence in the event she is being held against her will. We should park at the end of the road and hike up to the house so that he doesn't hear us coming."

Ed had to admit Martina appeared to know what she was doing. She was both a security consultant and a private investigator—not typical for anyone. Both were incredibly dangerous and tough jobs. Ed supposed he was lucky to have the backup, considering Renier had stayed behind due to a family emergency. But even if he had come along, Renier was three months from retirement and wasn't what you'd call *fit*. Ed doubted his partner would have been able to hike in the best of conditions let alone off-trail during a snowfall. He would've been near useless in this situation. "Sounds like a plan. When will your guys be in position?"

Martina nodded. "I sent them a message when we were

driving through Sacramento. They should be scattered in the surrounding areas, waiting for my signal."

Was she ex-military? Special ops? Who was Martina Monroe?

Martina tapped on the passenger window. "That's it. That's the road. Pull over."

He parked on the shoulder and he and Martina swiftly exited the car. Charlie had been sitting in the back. Silently, almost the entire ride.

Part of him still hoped they were walking into a teenage romance scenario and not what he feared most, which was that Selena was not there willingly. That she'd been taken.

Ed wondered if Zeek had gotten the idea that Selena didn't trust him or was trying to get away from him. Why hadn't Selena told Ed if she was trying to get away from Zeek? He could've helped and put her in touch with people who could protect her.

He popped the trunk and pulled out his flak jacket and slipped it on. Charlie and Martina joined him at the rear of the car. Martina and Ed quickly agreed on a plan of attack and hand signals.

Martina put her hand on Charlie's arm. "Maybe you should wait here. Detective Gates and I are trained. I don't want something to happen to you."

He shook his head. "No. She's my daughter. This is my fault. I should have tried to find her years ago. I should've never left. I'm gonna find her."

Martina hugged him and then pulled back. "Fine. Follow close behind and don't make a noise. Stay out of sight."

Ed stared at Martina. "It's go time." He mimicked zipping his mouth shut, nodded, and set off to hike up the road.

He surveyed from left to right. The winding road was outlined by mature pine trees draped in freshly fallen snow. He glanced over his shoulder and spotted Martina heading into the forest with Charlie trailing behind.

Ed continued on for ten minutes before he spotted the roof of a moderately sized A frame log cabin. On the other side of the house he saw Martina and Charlie. Martina was clearly motioning to Charlie to stay back and she was snooping in the windows.

Ed creeped up on the other side of the cabin as quietly as possible. He shimmied along the side of the house until he reached one of the windows. A quick glance confirmed a bedroom with a queen bed, two nightstands, a chair, and ... he froze. Was that rope on the bed? *Shit. Fuck.* He'd been right. She was in danger, if she was even still alive.

He crouched down and continued around the cabin. He reached the front corner and looked across to the other side, where Martina was squatting down. She signaled that she had a visual on two people and one had a gun. The look in Martina's eyes told him everything.

19

Selena felt the pressure of the gun on her forehead. Tears flowed down her temples. It was time to make peace with her life. Everything she had done wrong. The things she had done right. Maybe she deserved this. Her thoughts shifted as the gun slid off her face and Zeek sat up straight. "What the fuck was that?"

Selena opened her eyes wide. He was distracted. He thought he heard something, but it was probably just a deer. This was either an opportunity to fight for her life or a potential suicide mission. She turned to her right to see where the fork had landed and glanced up at the window. She thought she saw movement. Was somebody out there? She looked back to Zeek, who was no longer paying attention to her. He probably figured, rightly so, that she wasn't going anywhere with him pinned on top of her. She tried to reach for the fork but his eyes met hers. She would swear she saw Satan himself.

She pleaded, "Don't do this, Zeek. Please. I love you. You know that I love you."

He spat at her. "You're a stupid, lying bitch, just like all the others. Now you can be with the rest of them. Spoiler alert, it's not gonna turn out so great for you." Zeek aimed the gun and she closed her eyes and prayed. *Please God, if you're there, please don't let him kill me. I want to live. I want a life.*

A loud crash and bang forced her eyes open. In an instant, Zeek slumped over with blood oozing from his chest. His gun fell to the tile. Selena frantically pushed him off as if he were the Ebola virus. She rolled over onto all fours and was shocked to see Detective Gates and a woman rushing toward her and Zeek. Detective Gates grabbed the gun and hunched over Zeek.

The woman helped her up off the floor. The woman stared down at the fishing wire on Selena's ankle and then pulled out a knife from the leather pouch on her hip, flicked open the blade, and cut the wire before ushering Selena away from the kitchen.

The tall woman with dark, cropped hair studied her. "Selena, are you okay? Are you hurt?"

She shook her head. "I'm okay." *Sort of.*

The woman turned around and waved somebody over. Selena's heart stopped. "Dad?"

Her dad wrapped his arms around her. "Selena. I'm so happy to see you. I love you so much. I'm so sorry I wasn't there. I should've never left you. I've been trying to get my act together. I thought you'd hate me for leaving, so I stayed away. I'm so sorry."

She'd never seen her father cry before. Into his neck, she said, "I love you too."

Was this really happening? How had they found her? She wiped her face on her sleeve and stepped back. "I don't hate you. I'm so happy to see you. How did you find me?"

Her dad wiped at the corners of his eyes. "I found out that your mother died only a few days ago. This is Martina. She's my ... She's my fiancée, but she's also a private investigator. She's been working with the police to try to find you. Detective Gates explained to us the possible danger you were in. He said you didn't show up for an appointment on Monday and you hadn't gone to school. He couldn't reach you by phone."

Selena turned around to find Detective Gates approaching them. Beyond him, a pool of blood surrounded Zeek. She ran to Detective Gates and threw her arms around him and mumbled, "Thank you. Thank you. Thank you." She didn't know how long she clung to him before she stepped back and asked, "How did you know I was here?"

He grinned and she'd swear he had tears in his eyes. "It was a group effort. We've all been looking for you. You've met Martina? I'm not sure we would've found you in time if it wasn't for her."

Selena turned to face her ... future stepmother? "Is that true?"

"My firm helped get the intel quickly, but Detective Gates is the real hero. He's the one who broke down the door and shot Zeek, saving your life."

Moments ago, she thought she was going to die. She glanced up at the heroes who had saved her life. "I'm so sorry for causing so much trouble. I should've known better. I should've seen the signs. Growing up with Mom's steady stream of jerks, I should've known. I was so stupid." She looked away.

Detective Gates said, "You are not stupid, Selena. He was a master manipulator. Did you know that his last girlfriend ended up missing, presumed dead, and that he was a suspect?"

What? She shook her head.

Detective Gates forced her to look at him. "There was no way for you to have known. This is not your fault. You have no reason to apologize."

Martina put her hand on Selena's shoulder. "Detective Gates is right. You're not stupid. From what I hear, not by a long shot. In my line of work, I see this happen so often—*too often*. It happens to smart, not-so-bright, young, old, rich, poor, white, black, and purple people. It's not your fault. Zeek was a predator and he preyed on you. You can't blame yourself. These predators know how to blend in and disguise themselves. It always starts out wonderful and loving and then something happens for them to show their true selves, whether it's because they believe they can get away with it or because the abuser feels threatened, like I'm guessing Zeek did."

Selena didn't respond. If that was all true, why did she feel like such a fool?

In the distance sirens sang out. Selena glanced over her shoulder where Zeek's body lay crumpled. A mixture of heartbreak and relief filled her. She thought she had loved him and that he loved her. She'd thought he was a good catch. Smart, funny, and cute. His true colors were revealed too late. A monster who thought women were his property. How could she ever trust another man, or her own judgement, again?

20

CHRISTMAS EVE

Selena was folding laundry in her brand-new bedroom when she heard the doorbell ring. She set down the t-shirt she had in her hands and hurried down the hall to the front door. She climbed up on her tiptoes, looked through the peephole, and smiled.

She opened the door. On her front porch stood Detective Gates holding a large cardboard box. "Merry Christmas Eve! C'mon in." She stepped back making room for him to enter.

He said, "Merry Christmas to you too, Selena. Where can I put this?"

"You can bring it in the dining room, Dad and Martina are in there too." She led him down the hall and veered left into the dining room where her father and Martina sat at a large oval table with a poinsettia in the center.

Martina and Charlie stood up and shook the detective's hand. Martina said, "It's good to see you, Detective. Thank you for coming over tonight. You didn't have to do that on Christmas Eve, but we're definitely happy to see you."

Detective Gates turned a pale shade of pink. "Not a problem, it was on my way home. I thought Selena might like her things now that we've released Zeek's apartment. Also, we have more information about Zeek I'd like to share. It's a bit disturbing, but, Selena, I think it's important for you to hear. I also have some good news to tell you. Why don't you go ahead and sit down."

Selena took a chair and sat down apprehensively. She didn't know what he was about to tell her. It had been nine days since she'd almost been killed. So much had happened since then. Martina and her Dad had welcomed her into their home with open arms. Martina had insisted that she move in right away and had even found her a counselor to talk to about her experience. She knew it would be a long time before she could trust another man, but it was okay. She had more important things to focus on.

Selena had never met anybody quite like Martina before. A woman who was strong, independent, and had zero hesitation in fighting the bad guys. Selena had only known Martina for a short time, but she felt a strong connection to her, like they were destined to cross paths even if Martina wasn't engaged to her father. It was the first time Selena ever had a real role model to look up to. She hadn't told Martina this, but Selena had decided on a new career path because of her.

A few days ago, Martina had even taken her shopping to pick out linens and decorations for her new room. She was so grateful that her dad and Martina had come into her life. Selena wondered if all the bad stuff hadn't happened—her mother's death or her own near death— would she be where she was now? Maybe she had to go through that horrible nightmare to have this beautiful family and home. It was more than she'd ever dreamed of, because she didn't know what a loving home looked like. So yes, she did want to know more about Zeek, because if it wasn't for him she wasn't quite sure she'd be sitting at this table right now. And there was nowhere else she'd rather be. She nodded at Detective Gates. "I want to know." She steadied herself, bracing for the worst.

He said, "After searching the apartment and his parents' cabin, we found evidence connected to two other missing girls. One was the girlfriend we knew was missing and connected to him. The second was another female student who had gone missing during his first year at UC Berkeley. The evidence uncovered led us to two grave sites near the cabin. They found both women."

Selena covered her mouth with her hand and looked down. She had fallen in love with and dated a murderer. *A murderer.* The monster hiding behind a killer smile and warm embrace. She moved her hand back to her lap and looked up at Detective Gates. "Have their families been told?"

He gave her a reassuring smile. "Yes. Although devastated, they were relieved to finally have closure after so long. They can now bury their loved one and begin the healing process. Which in itself is a gift. We were able to give that gift to those families because of you. Because of your bravery. Because you fought Zeek. Because you came to me and gave me clues that something was wrong. Because of you, we found those girls. So please don't think everything you went through was for nothing."

She thought about that. She didn't think she really deserved the credit he was giving her. Sure, she'd hinted that she didn't think that Zeek wanted to be around law enforcement, and if it weren't for Detective Gates, she would be dead and the graves never would've been found. So maybe it was partly true. Because of her situation, two families received closure and could now bury their loved ones. There was something remarkable about that. That such horrible ugliness could bring a little bit of light to two other families.

"Thank you for sharing that with me. I'm glad you were able to find them."

Detective Gates gave her a lopsided grin. "You are very welcome. I also have some good news that I wanted to share right away. Fox, actual name Fletcher Peterson, agreed to a plea deal this morning. With the physical evidence against him, your statements, and your identification of him, the district attorney had a lot to work with. They were going to charge him with capital murder, which meant he could have received the death penalty. The deal he accepted gives him life in prison without the possibility of parole, in lieu of the death penalty. He will be spending the rest of his life in prison."

Selena's eyes widened. "So, he'll never get out?"

Detective Gates's hazel eyes sparkled. "Never."

Tears streamed down Selena's cheeks. "Thank you. Thank you so much for getting justice for my mom."

Martina wrapped her arm around Selena as she cried quietly. Her dad jumped up and dashed out of the room and returned with a box of tissues. Martina grabbed them from him and handed a single tissue to Selena. Selena calmed herself and wiped her eyes. Despite all her faults, Selena missed her mother and knew that she probably always would.

Martina spoke up. "Detective, my daughter, Zoey, will be home soon, she's been away at at school, but she's coming home tonight to celebrate Christmas with us. We'd love for you to stay and join us for dinner."

Detective Gates popped up out of his chair. "I appreciate the offer, but my wife and mother-in-law are at home cooking up our own celebration. I should get going, but I'd like to wish all of you a very Merry Christmas."

Selena pushed back her chair and stood up. "I'll walk you out."

The detective, Charlie, and Martina said their goodbyes and Merry Christmases.

At the door, Selena said, "I want to thank you for everything you did for me. I know you went above and beyond, and I don't think I'd be alive today if it wasn't for you. You not only brought justice for my mother, but you also saved my life. I don't know how I can ever repay you." She sniffed away the tears that were coming. Why did she always cry in front of this person? *It was super annoying.*

He smiled warmly. "I was just doing my job, Selena. But I'm glad I was able to help. I'm glad you're safe and sound. I want to wish you the best in your studies, your future. I'm sure you'll go far, I have no doubt. Merry Christmas."

Selena shook off some of her tears and wiped her face with the back of her hand. "Merry Christmas, Detective Gates." She shut the door and turned back toward her family. Warmth filled every particle inside her. Between her future stepmother who was a total badass, the detective who had watched her back, and her loving father, she had never felt more cared for.

Later that night, they sat in the living room, admiring the seven-foot-tall Christmas tree lit up with sparkling lights and colorful ornaments. Selena sipped her hot cocoa while sitting next to her future stepsister. Across from them, her father and future stepmother held hands as they laughed at whatever inside joke they shared.

"So, Selena, Mom says you're hoping to get into San Francisco University. Have you thought about majors yet?" Zoey asked.

"Well, I had planned on maybe going into nursing or medicine but after everything, I'm now leaning more towards criminal justice and think maybe I'll go into law enforcement or private investigations or something like that. I want to help people."

Martina cocked her head. "I didn't know that. That's great. You know, if you'd like a part-time job, we could use you down at the office. You'd get a chance to see how things work in the world of security and private investigations."

Selena beamed at Martina. "I would love that! Oh my gosh, thank you." She couldn't believe she'd be a part of a real-life investigative team. She didn't need a single wrapped gift, she already had everything she could possibly have asked for.

Martina smiled. "Great. I'll put together a plan when I get back in the office next week."

Selena grinned at her and then she dropped her gaze to the small round diamond on Martina's finger. "When do you two plan on getting married?"

Martina and her dad exchanged glances. "Well, we were thinking of the spring, maybe March, when Zoey will be home for spring break. Also, there is something we wanted to ask both of you. Zoey, would you be my maid of honor?"

Zoey's eyes widened. "Yes, of course!"

Charlie sat up straight. "And Selena, I'd would like you to be my best woman. Will you?"

"Best woman?" Selena asked.

Charlie explained, "It's kind of like a best man, but you're a woman, so a best woman."

"Yes! I'd love to! Do I wear a tux or a dress?"

Charlie smiled. "Anything you want."

Selena nodded. "Cool."

When she'd heard the story of how Martina and her father had met it made her wonder if his addiction was a lot like the nightmare she had just gone through. He had to go to a place of darkness to find his light. Martina and Charlie had met in rehab. Martina was a volunteer and ten years sober while Charlie was a patient. Apparently, they'd fallen in love, but rules said they couldn't be in a relationship. After he'd passed his one year of being drug-free, he'd asked her on a date and the rest was history. Selena was proud of her dad for getting clean. On more than one occasion she had watched him flip his two-year chip between his fingers. She thought her dad was proud of himself too. As he should be.

She looked across the room at the fireplace that displayed four stockings decorated with names written in red glitter. *Martina. Charlie. Zoey. Selena.* She was overwhelmed by the love in that room. For the first time in her life, she had a real home and a family. A future. Not only was she determined to become the strongest person, mentally and physically, that she could be, but she also vowed to never, ever be a victim again.

A NOTE FROM H.K. CHRISTIE

When I started this project, I thought I knew a decent amount about domestic violence. I listen to a lot of true crime podcasts and watch a lot of documentaries where domestic violence is usually a factor. But for *Not Like Her*, I wanted to learn more about the intricacies of domestic violence (intimate partner violence) to portray a more realistic story for Selena and her mother.

What I found was that domestic violence is a much more complex topic than I had anticipated. It happens more than you'd think and to all demographics and socioeconomic statuses.

As you recall, in the story of Selena and Zeek, the courtship was fast, Zeek never referred to Selena by her name, only 'babe', and lied about his background. He attempted to isolate her by insisting she quit her job and monopolized all of her time. These are all typical red flags of an abusive relationship. Zeek didn't need to tie Selena to a bed to abuse her - it started before that. Abuse isn't limited to physical bruises.

Instead of writing a full manifesto on the topic (which would read more like me ranting and raving), I encourage you to read about the topic either on the website for the **National Domestic Violence Hotline** or other online resources or at your local library.

Through awareness we can help prevent intimate partner violence.

If you find yourself in a relationship similar to Selena and Zeek's, or are in an abusive situation there are resources available at the website for:

National Domestic Violence Hotline

Safety Alert: Computer use can be monitored and is impossible to completely clear. If you are afraid your internet usage might be monitored, call the **National Domestic Violence Hotline at 1–800–799–7233** instead of using your computer.

THANK YOU!

Thank you for reading *Not Like Her*! I hope you enjoyed reading it as much as I loved writing it. If you did, I would greatly appreciate if you could post a short review.

Reviews are crucial for any author and can make a huge difference in visibility of current and future works. Reviews allow us to continue doing what we love, *writing stories.* Not to mention, I would be forever grateful!

To leave a review, go to the webpage for *Not Like Her* and write your review.

Thank you!

ALSO BY H.K. CHRISTIE

The Selena Bailey Novella Series

If you enjoyed, *Not Like Her,* get the rest of the series today.

One In Five, Book 2

On The Rise, Book 3

The Unbreakable Series

The Unbreakable Series is a heart-warming women's fiction series, inspired by true events. If you like journeys of self-discovery, wounded heroines, and laugh-or-cry moments, you'll love the Unbreakable Series

We Can't Be Broken, Book 0

Where I'm Supposed To Be, Book 1

Change of Plans, Book 2

JOIN H.K. CHRISTIE'S READER'S CLUB

Join my reader club to be the first to hear about upcoming novels, new releases, giveaways, promotions, and more!

It's completely free to sign up and you'll never be spammed by me, you can opt out easily at any time.

To sign up go to
www.authorhkchristie.com

ABOUT THE AUTHOR

H.K. Christie is the author of compelling stories about unbreakable women.

When not working on her latest novel, she can be found eating, drinking, hiking, or playing with her new 9 year old rescue pup, Founders.

She is a native and current resident of the San Francisco Bay Area and a two time graduate of Saint Mary's College of California.

www.authorhkchristie.com

ACKNOWLEDGMENTS

I want to thank my bad-ass niece, Gianna Lazzarini, for working with me to better understand the mind and life of a high school senior. It was a tremendous help in ensuring that Selena didn't sound like a middle-aged woman! My sincerest thank you!

A special thank you to Police Officer Gabe Irving for letting me tag along for the evening (fighting crime!) and for the interesting and insightful discussions around violence against women. It was a truly fascinating evening and I learned so much. My most sincere thank you.

I'd like to thank my *Super Elite Level* beta readers: Juliann Brown & Jennifer Jarrett. Thank you for the continued encouragement, support, and invaluable feedback.

I'd like to thank my additional beta readers & critiquers: Barbara Carson, Anne Kasaba, and Robin Samuels. Your feedback is invaluable. Thank you!

A big thank you to Nicole Nugent for the copy edit.

I'd like to thank Suzana Stankovic who designed the cover. You did an amazing job with the cover - once again. Your unrelenting patience is appreciated. Thank you!

Last, but certainly not least, a special thank you to my

husband, Jon, for not only performing the proof read, but also for listening to me ranting and raving about the patriarchy every time I finished reading something new about intimate partner violence. At this point in our relationship, he's basically a candidate for sainthood.